# Also by Yawatta Hosby

One By One
Something's Amiss
Twisted Obsession
Six Plus One
Perfect Little Murder
Two Book Boxset
Urban Legends

Watch for more at yawattahosbysbooks.wordp.

# ONE BY ONE
Yawatta Hosby

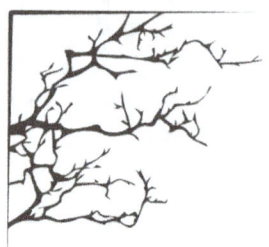

# Copyright Page

One By One

By Yawatta Hosby

Book Cover: James at GoOnWrite.com

Editor: Jim Baroni

Published by: Dream Snatcher Press in the United States

This story is a work of fiction. Names, characters, and incidents are either products of the author's imagination or are used fictitiously. Any resemblance to actual events, locales, organizations or persons, living or dead, is entirely coincidental.

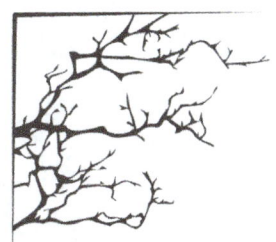

# Dedication

To Mrs. Kirby, my first creative writing teacher. Thank you for believing in me and encouraging me to write fiction, besides just drawing.

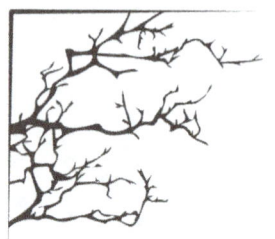

# Acknowledgments

I would like to thank my family and friends for their support. I'd also like to thank my blogging buddies and other writing friends. Because of you, I'm getting out of writing as just a hobby.

I'd like to thank Melissa and Robin. I wouldn't have *One By One* created if we didn't participate in NaNoWriMo together. After having fun with that writing challenge, it took me over a year to publish this book. Thank you Melissa for being my critique partner besides just my writing buddy. It's always fun when we go on our mini-adventures. I'd also like to thank my beta-readers, Beth and Mike E. Because of you, I was able to see if my mystery thriller had enough red-herrings and if the plot and characters were interesting enough to get through.

I would also like to thank my cover design artist, James (www.goonwrite.com). Thanks for taking a chance on a debut author. Last but not least, I'd like to thank my horror author friend, Jim Baroni (www.jtbaroni.com). If he wouldn't have offered to edit my manuscript, then *One By One* would still only be a Microsoft Word document on my computer instead of a book for sale.

Thank you for supporting my dreams. You'll never know how much that truly means to me.

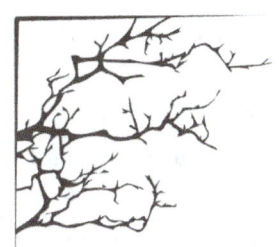

# Chapter One

Kenan pounded on the door. Still no answer. "Rae, I know you're in there. Your car's out front. Let me in." He waited, then knocked again. He grabbed his keys out of his navy blue hoodie pocket and let himself into his sister's one bedroom apartment.

Kenan found Rae asleep in bed. Instead of wearing pajamas, she had on red shorts and a yellow top, so she hadn't slept the day away. Well, maybe the morning, he reasoned, but now, it was mid-afternoon. He lifted the sleeping pill container off her nightstand and examined it. Rae's psychological need for the tablets was never consistent; some weeks she'd need to take one every night. Other times she'd sleep like a baby without the help of prescriptions. The container was almost empty; maybe they should make a pit stop to Rite-Aide first to fill it. If she had taken a pill recently, no wonder she was knocked out and didn't answer the door. He felt better knowing that Rae wasn't purposely avoiding him.

He picked up *50 Shades of Grey* and skimmed through the pages. A bookmark—photo of him, Rae, their mom and dad standing on the wraparound porch at the cabin—surfaced. A forest was nestled in the valley in the background. Kenan took a deep breath and caressed it with his finger. He remembered that day as if it were yesterday. They had just finished swimming at the lake; his dad's brother and cousins were on their way home before snapping the photo.

Two hours after the photo was taken...

Kenan shook his head, attempting to erase his memory. He put the photo back where he found it and set the book on the nightstand.

If he had his way, nothing tragic would have happened during their teen years. Kenan and his sister wouldn't have lost their parents. They would have been born to a bigger family, so they could've had a better support system. Kenan could handle depression, but he feared for Rae. How much more of a bad deck could she handle?

He searched the room, looking for an overnight bag but didn't find one. He frowned and sat on the blue carpeted floor, facing the bed to continue watching his sister sleep. She looked so peaceful.

Since last week, she'd been telling everyone that she wasn't joining them at the cabin. She was on board to go to the beach for a three-day weekend until the cabin was mentioned. Even if it'd only be a short period of time, Rae couldn't stand the thought of putting herself through that. Being self-absorbed, Naomi, one of her best friends, kept pressing the issue, making things about herself, about her feelings, which got the two ladies into a shouting match. He was proud that Rae held her own; however, the girls hadn't spoken since. He felt it was time to step in and be the mediator—life was too short to end long-term friendships over petty dramas.

Kenan pulled his phone out of his jean pocket and texted his best friend, Tobey: *She's asleep. Need more time. Hang out someplace for a while then we'll meet you guys.*

He received a reply: *Ok, see you soon.*

Kenan sighed, placing his phone on the floor. With brown eyes, he was average height with a stocky build. His afro was uncombed and his scruff was untamed. If Kenan didn't have a cute face, strangers may mistake him for homeless. He was emotionally drained because he felt horrible that Rae was hurting. He'd do anything to take her pain away. That was actually an understatement. He'd do everything possible.

Eventually, Rae yawned and lay on her side. Stretching, she asked, "How long have you been here?"

"Not long." Kenan smiled. "Will you do me a favor?"

"I'm not going." She folded her arms across her chest.

The sky lit up with a lightning bolt, and the windows rattled. The rain hitting the ceiling sounded like firecrackers going off. "Look it's storming. It's not a good time to travel anywhere." She sat up in bed. One side of her hair was flat where she had been lying on it while the other half had her natural curls swinging all over the place.

Kenan covered his mouth to hide a grin.

"What's funny?" she asked.

He pointed to her head. Rae must have got the message loud and clear; she jumped to the mirror and brushed her brown with red highlights afro into a style. Rae was only five-three, had brown eyes and a ruler shape body. The tattoo of a dreamcatcher on her right hand was the most spontaneous thing she had ever done.

"Come on, Rae. It's me, your big brother, Kenan. I wouldn't ask you to do something that I thought you couldn't handle. Please. I need you there. I can't handle this alone."

Rae slowly set the brush down onto the dark brown dresser; she looked at him through the mirror. She frowned and closed her eyes. "Don't handle it at all. Don't go."

"It's not that simple. That day haunts me every day whether I'm at the cabin or not. I might as well go to try and get closure or something. It'll be good for us. Let that guy sign the deed then it's his. We'd eventually sale that property and never have to visit it again."

"Can't Uncle John just do it?"

"No, it has to be the property owners, a.k.a. me and you."

"We can sign it then mail it to him."

"No, Rae. We have to be there. What if the deed got lost in the mail?"

Rae shrugged her shoulders. "We can fax it or hire a real estate agent."

"The guy needs the original, not a copy. Therefore, we have to physically hand the paper over to him, not fax it. I can't afford to hire an agent, neither can you."

"Kenan—"

"Rae, I love you. I'd never ask you to do this if I didn't think you couldn't handle it. We can finally get closure. All our friends will be there to support us, then we can go on our merry way to enjoy ourselves at the beach. We'll be at the cabin for an hour tops." Kenan placed his hands together in a pleading fashion. "What do I have to do to get you to agree?"

She fell silent, wiping a tear from her eye.

Kenan closed his eyes. "This guy finally agreed to buy the place. I'm sorry that it has to be today; it's the only time he's free. Otherwise, I would've never agreed to it. We're heading to Virginia anyway. Just one pit stop, Rae. One pit stop that won't even take an hour. Then it's over. It's finally over." He sighed. "Rae, it'll hurt if I have to go alone. I need you there to hold it together...our vacation home used to be our favorite spot until those monsters ruined every-thing. Don't let them keep winning."

"I haven't packed."

"I can wait."

Rae slowly took clothes out of her drawer and stuffed them in her red back-pack.

Kenan texted: *Head back. We're ready.*

"Who you talking to?"

"Tobey." He put the phone back in his pocket and fidgeted with his fingers.

"Are you sure you wanna go? It's never too late to back out," she asked in a concerned fashion, focusing on his hands.

Kenan gulped; he hid his hands in his sleeve. "I'm okay as long as you're there. Do you need more sleeping pills?"

"No, I'll be all right. So who's all going?"

He ran down the list. Rae rolled her eyes at the mention of Naomi's name, which caused Kenan to smirk.

"I'm not driving three hours with Naomi," she demanded.

"Anymore requests?"

"I'm serious, Kenan. I can't deal with her."

He wondered if Rae would change her tune if her friend were gone forever. Not one person's day on earth was guaranteed. What if one day Naomi just vanished? Or died in a terrible accident? Would his sister feel guilty about not making up with her? Would she feel numb? There was plenty of time to explore that concept, so Kenan didn't plan to rush the reconciliation just yet. "You'll be 'Naomi free' for our road trip."

Rae sighed. "Don't road trips consist of going places where everyone in the car wants to travel to?"

"Not necessarily...we should go." Kenan stood up and ran his hands over his clothes to smooth them out, knocking pieces of lint from the carpet that stayed on the fabric.

He headed toward the door. He turned around when he didn't hear foot-steps behind him. Rae still remained on the edge of her bed, staring at the wall. He ambled back and grabbed her book bag. He sat close to her. He wrapped his arms around her shoulder. She sobbed.

Soon, Rae's pain would be gone. He'd make sure of it.

THE PARKING LOT WAS pretty empty, although many families resided in Rae's apartment building. She figured most of them were probably on their way to enjoy the Fourth of July weekend with relatives. Not having to face their pasts.

Rae stood under the umbrella near Tobey. His quiet and peaceful nature was a good influence on her brother. Tobey soared past six-three with broad shoulders and a quarterback body frame, especially a thick neck. His black stringy hair was cut short, and he had brown eyes. Years ago, they met when Kenan had moved to North Carolina; Kenan had convinced Tobey to visit his hometown, and Tobey stayed ever since. Her friends were scattered in groups near the two Jeeps. They were interacting with each other as if they weren't bothered getting wet.

"Who's that?" Rae asked Tobey as he put her belongings in the back of the Jeep. She pointed to the only stranger near the other rented vehicle. He looked like a model with his intense brown eyes, strong cheekbones, and wavy black hair that fell a little past his shoulders. The stranger was tall and lanky, but you could tell he had a six-pack under his shirt. His facial hair and eyebrows were sculpted to perfection on his tan skin.

Brady walked up to them and stood beside her. "Oh, that's Creepy Boy, who Marissa literally picked up minutes ago."

"Creepy Boy?"

"Yeah, there has to be a few screws loose when a girl asks you to drop everything to spend a three-day weekend on very short notice, and you say okey dokey without a care in the world." Brady rubbed the back of his neck. He wore a red v-neck and gray Capri shorts with his Ed Hardy sunglasses. There was an inside joke among the ladies that Brady followed Rae from college. They had lived in the same dorm, in fact, on the same floor. After graduation, Brady miraculously received a job offer in the good ole eastern panhandle of West Virginia. Harpers Ferry was only a few minutes away from Charles Town where she lived.

No one could deny that Brady was attractive. His tall and lanky body never tanned; he always joked that his Irish heritage was to blame. He had dark blue eyes and shaggy black hair that framed his oval face. She felt lucky to have Brady as a friend even though he acted as if he wanted to reach the next level. If he didn't flirt with every female who breathed, if he acted as though he had standards, then maybe she would take him more seriously.

Tobey grinned. All three looked at Adam, who held hands with Marissa. What was she thinking, bringing a stranger with them? Could he be trusted? Unlike Rae, Marissa was fearless. She kept trying to teach her childhood friend that life was too short not to take risks, but Rae had a habit of not listening. Marissa had light blue eyes and a long, narrow face. Her hair had a side-swept bang and the length went well past her back; it was golden blonde on top and light brown underneath. She was medium-height and pretty skinny. Her olive skin tone was always tanned.

Brady rolled his eyes when Logan, Kenan's roommate, approached them. Logan had light green eyes and kissable full lips that looked beautiful against his dark brown skin. He was medium-height and built like a football player. Logan placed his hand on the bottom of Rae's back, then quickly removed it. "You made it." He smiled.

"You know I can never say no to Kenan."

He laughed. "One day."

Brady frowned; Rae blushed. She had a secret crush on Logan and hoped she wasn't being obvious. She didn't want to hurt Brady's feelings. Plus, she didn't want to make a fool of herself. It was more than likely that Logan only thought of her as 'Kenan's younger sister.'

Brady winked. "Can you say no to me?"

She grinned. "Never."

Logan sneered as Brady wrapped his arms around Rae. She laughed to ease the tension. "I'm happy that you guys are coming too. I'll need as many happy faces as possible to get me through this."

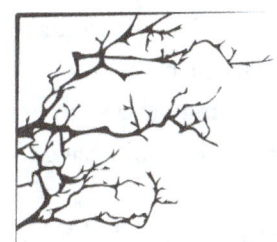

# Chapter Two

Brady frowned. "This sucks. I wanted to be in the other car."

"Why didn't you get in?" Selma asked. She sported a Victoria's Secret PINK hoodie and PINK sweatpants. Her casual look was heightened with her brown hair in a ponytail. With light green eyes, she stood at only five-four and had plenty of men mesmerized with her curvy hips and big breasts.

"Because he wanted to make our lives miserable." Naomi rolled her eyes, staring out the window. She had brown doe-like eyes, a heart-shape face always covered with make-up. Her strong cheekbones were highlighted by her pixie cut. She was pretty tall with attractive proportions, resembling a print ad model. They passed red/white barns, cows standing in fields, and shadows of mountains at a far away distance, which resembled a background in a Norman Rockwell painting.

Brady decided to change the subject. "Does anyone else think it's strange that Marissa is bringing some stranger with us on our bonding trip?"

"What happened with that again?" Kenan asked.

"The sleaze picked him up in the parking lot of Dairy Queen." Selma laughed. "I'm sure he's only tagging along for an easy lay."

"She's not a sleaze." Kenan's hands gripped tighter on the steering wheel.

Selma gave him an icy glare. "She cheated on you."

Kenan refused to respond; he watched the road ahead. She looked out the window and folded her arms across her chest.

"Do you know A-dumb?" Brady asked Naomi. She quickly shook her head, conveying that she couldn't bring herself to lowering her standards and talking to *commoners*.

Brady thought it was strange that no one knew who this guy was. Maybe he was older or younger than they were? Since he didn't trust Adam, he'd interrogate him with questions. He'd have to prove himself before Brady would sleep in the same room as the stranger. He, Marissa, Rae, and Logan were supposed to share a room while the couples had their own suite. Adam would have to fork over his own money and buy his own room with Marissa at the hotel.

If Brady had to, he'd spend the night in his own room and maybe try to persuade Rae to join him. Nah. She wouldn't fall for that line. He would have to try something else.

It sucked that she was spending three hours with Logan. She would be too nice to tell him to shut up if he got on her nerves. Besides, he probably smelled like a wet dog, and the storm wouldn't allow them to roll down their windows. If only Brady was there to intervene. It'd be cool to get Kenan's opinion of who'd fit better with his sister. Her friend or his roommate. Knowing him, Kenan would probably say neither, Brady laughed to himself.

Later, Brady continued to complain. First, it was too hot in the Jeep. Second, he forgot his guitar at the house, said he needed something to do all weekend, which Kenan refused to turn around—an hour already into the trip. Then he criticized Adam's intentions again. He was relentless, not caring if anyone was listening to his tirade or not.

"Will you shut the hell up?" Naomi ordered, never taking her eyes off the window. She scooted as close to the edge of the seat as possible.

"I'm just saying. It's really weird that this guy tagged along, just came without letting anyone know first. No text or call, warning anyone. What kind of loser is he to not have any obligations for three whole days?"

"We get it. You don't like him," Kenan said.

Brady slapped his head in frustration. "Am I the only one thinking clearly? That *stranger* seems suspicious, and if we don't watch our backs, we all may be killed in our sleep by Psycho Boy."

"You sound like a jealous ex. Do you have a crush on Marissa?" Selma asked, surprisingly, as though no one could develop feelings for her 'rival.' Brady didn't understand why the two women couldn't get along. Kenan had clearly moved on with Selma, so why did she still feel threatened by Marissa? At least Brady assumed that was the reason she always got her digs in.

Now would be a great opportunity to say it was Rae, who he had feelings for. If only he knew that Kenan would have his back. The last thing he needed was to be dropped off on the side of the road in the country. Brady was a pretty boy, but maybe not good-looking enough to have someone allow him to hitchhike in their car.

If only he was a girl, then he'd have a better chance of getting a ride. If anyone were to pass him now, they'd probably think he was dangerous. But Brady couldn't hurt a fly. Or could he? He'd never been tested far enough to prove that theory.

He decided to play it safe. "Nah, we're cool, but nah."

"I mean it would've worked out perfectly. You and Marissa off to do your own thing; Rae and Logan off to do their own thing." Selma ignored his earlier remark. That was the thing with Selma—her focus was so narrow that once she had an idea put into her head, it was hard for her to grasp a different outcome even if the evidence was placed right in front of her face. There could be a ten-hour lecture, verbalizing hardcore facts of why she was wrong, and she'd still think she was right.

"There's nothing going on between Logan and my sister." Kenan shook his head while his girlfriend gave him a doubted glance. He ignored the gesture, looking straight ahead. "If anything, I'd rather her and Brady get together if she dated anyone in our group."

Brady's ears perked up.

Of course, Naomi had to rain on his parade. "Ew, never gonna happen."

"Why not?" Brady asked defensively.

"Because she has taste."

"Well, she can't date my boy, Logan, because I'd have to kick his ass if the relationship didn't work out. I'd have to pick sides and everything would get messy. I'd lose a friend and a roommate in the process, all because he couldn't keep his dick in his pants." Kenan smirked. "I'd rather she dated someone like Brady. That way I wouldn't feel guilty having to destroy his existence if he broke my little sister's heart."

Brady gulped, getting the message loud and clear. Kenan had implied that they weren't friends, weren't boys, weren't brothers from another mother, weren't amigos. Brady knew they weren't close, but Kenan didn't have to call him out like that.

However, on the plus side, he gave him permission to pursue Rae. Might as well get tips. Brady fidgeted with his hands. "How could I win her over?"

"Do you have a crush on Rae?" Selma smiled and moved her body, so she could face him in the back seat. She had an enlightened and accepting facial expression.

Brady's cheeks turned red. "What do you think?"

Selma clapped, her green eyes widened with delight. "Oh my gosh, you do! How cute is that?" She couldn't stop smiling. "You know how you have a habit of flirting with any girl who breathes. Well, you should stop that and only focus on Rae. That way she'd take you seriously."

He bookmarked that suggestion in his memory like it was his favorite website on his computer. He sneaked a peek at Kenan, who glanced at him in the rearview mirror. Kenan looked serious, winked, then grinned, quickly eyeing the road again.

Should he take that as a good sign?

Did Kenan just show happiness for Brady? Or was he plotting to embarrass Brady this weekend?

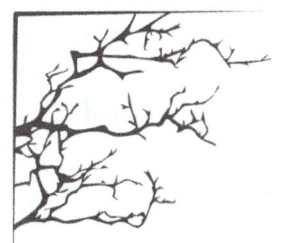

# Chapter Three

The Jeeps were parked outside of an old-fashioned style ma and pa filling station. At the two-hour mark, they had all agreed to stop for a restroom break and to fill up their gas tanks. Tobey had no idea what part of Virginia he was in, but it was more country than his hometown. Only woods covered the other side of the road. There weren't any houses for miles and miles. The store looked like an old, abandoned building with gray paint chipping off the rotten wood near the front entrance. One with two broken down pumps with nothing but dust and dead flies on the shelves. With no concrete parking lot, the Jeeps were covered in dust by the debris and dirt flying up from the wheels turning on the ground.

The forest across the street reminded Tobey of his home in North Carolina, reminiscent of a mansion with maids and servants. Coming from a huge family, he was forced to share a room. When they were allowed to play outside, the backyard was nothing but trees. A forest not barricaded by a fence. The porch wrapped around the entire mansion. Tobey had been smart to find secret hiding places among the yard, a place to sit and think for hours and hours.

Kenan leaned against the Jeep while Tobey pumped gas. They stood alone. "Brady made a good point in the car. What if Adam is dangerous?"

Tobey cracked his neck. "We could take him," he said matter-of-factly. Not cocky. Not aggressively. He wasn't the kind of guy to jump into random fights or shouting matches to prove his manhood, but if he needed to protect himself or loved ones, that wouldn't be a problem for him.

Within the few minutes he spent outside, Tobey hadn't noticed any cars pull into the parking lot or drive past. Was this a ghost town? One of those places where crazy locals took turns tormenting, terrorizing, and murdering outsiders, who foolishly stopped in this No Name, NoHintOfItOnAMap town? Or worse yet, what if the town was full of racists?

He pulled his cell phone out from his brown/blue plaid shorts pocket, and sighed in relief when he noticed the energy bar was full. Thank God! He felt secure knowing he had service in case rednecks or any other crazies tried to attack them.

"Hey, dude. Put that away; you want us to blow up."

Tobey laughed. "That's only if the car engine is on."

AT THE CHECKOUT COUNTER, Adam bought snacks and drinks for the 'ladies.' He figured treating them was the least he could do to thank them for being so hot and sexy. Not one ugly chick in the bunch! He'd have to introduce Rae, Naomi, and Selma to his boys. Birds of a feather flock together—they were probably easy like Marissa.

Boyfriend or not, some, no all, women knew how to successfully cheat on their man. They were clever and manipulative in that way. Guys were either too stupid or braggarts, and that's why they always got caught.

Adam enjoyed being the center of female attention. Who knew? If he could please Marissa in the sack, she may brag to her friends, then they'd want to ride him too. He'd be sure to be cool with it, if they could sneak off. The last thing Adam needed was to have four guys jump him. He realized since moving to West Virginia, country bumpkins only shared one brain cell. They fought out any problems to solve them; they were too dumb to communicate effectively.

Adam was from Los Angeles and dreaded every second of his decision moving to the east coast. What had he been thinking five years ago? But then again, most, no all, girls in L.A. were fake, plastic, gold diggers who were either celebrity's daughters, future porn stars, or wannabe actresses too lazy to take acting classes. Oh, he couldn't forget supermodels. At least in West Virginia, he could spend less money while still getting laid. It was a nice savings arrangement. And he sensed that these Appalachian girls were not faking their orgasms.

Outside, he and the ladies stood under the trees for shade to escape the sunrays beaming down on them. Adam, who wore a green Ralph Lauren buttoned shirt and khakis, laughed to himself; he assumed the other guys were jealous of him for stealing the females' attention. He could picture the guys huddled in a corner. 'Me Big Dummy. Me Jealous Because Me Girl Is Talking To Hot Guy. No Interaction With Opposite Sex. Me Must Pound My Chest Then Pound The Guy's Head In.'

Girls were gullible, so he thought it'd be a good idea to scare them. With a serious facial expression, he said, "Marissa should have done a background check on me before inviting me with you guys."

"Why?" Naomi asked, wide-eyed.

He gave a sinister smile. "Because I'm crazy."

The girls shared a look of oh-no-he-didn't. Marissa chuckled, hitting Adam on the arm. "Stop playing like that. Don't be a douche."

"I'm not being a douche. I'm being myself."

"No you aren't."

Adam smirked. "How would you know, Marissa? You've known me for less than three-hours." He wagged his finger in front of her face, causing her to slap it away. "Didn't your mom ever teach you not to talk—let alone pick up—strangers?"

Marissa rolled her eyes and folded her arms across her chest. Oh yeah, she was into him. She was turned on right now. Adam never understood women. Why did they want jerks when they could have a nice guy? Bad boys ruled!

Before he could tell them he was joking, Brady, skepticism plastered on his face, walked over and interrupted his social hour. Apparently, his boys must have sent him over as their spokesperson. Like clockwork, Brady went into third degree questioning. "Where are you from, Adam?" Brady stared directly into Adam's eyes.

"Florida," Adam lied, quickly thinking on his feet. He could handle this putz.

"Last I checked, people are from cities within a state. Like me, I'm from Pittsburgh, Pennsylvania. So. You. Are. From?"

"The. Ever. Glades. Florida." Maybe if these hillbillies thought Adam was a country fellow, then they'd cut him some slack.

"Ever been to a swamp tour?" Rae asked.

"A couple of times. My uncle actually organizes tours down on the swamp." Might as well go all out with the lie.

Brady cracked his knuckles. "How old are you?"

"Thirty," he fibbed again.

"Congratulations, Marissa, you snagged an older man." Naomi grabbed her friend's hand, raising it in mock triumph. She gave Rae a spiteful look then left.

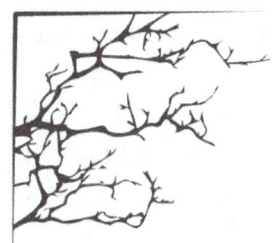

# Chapter Four

Rae peered out the window. They were back on the road. Since she didn't appreciate Adam's joke or the way Marissa stood up for him, she decided to switch rides. Naomi had been all too pleased to join her boyfriend, Tobey. Rae rolled her eyes because Naomi probably thought she did her a favor. Absolutely not! She was still highly pissed; Naomi wouldn't get out of this without an apology.

Selma said, "Rae, doesn't Brady have the bluest eyes you've ever seen? I've been around him so long, but now is the first time I truly noticed how deep blue they are, like the sea."

That was random.

"Thanks for saying my eyes are unmemorable," Brady said.

"What do you mean?" Selma gave a questioned look. "I was giving you a compliment."

"Not if you've been around me for a while now—what, a couple of years—and only today you notice my sexy eyes. Definitely not a compliment."

"You know what I meant."

"Doesn't matter what you think...only what Rae thinks. She's the only opinion I care about."

Rae looked into his beautiful oval eyes. She studied them, blushing. He looked her up and down. "I'll give you a ten out of ten." She smiled.

"And, I'll give you a twenty out of ten." Brady winked.

"Thank you."

Selma and Kenan grinned, then her brother stated, "Rae, you should show Brady the Orgasm Tree."

"Sounds kinky. Is it a lover's spot?" Selma asked.

In fact, it was. Rae blushed. She had never visited the popular spot, but Kenan had snuck there every so often when he was dating the neighbor's daughter. The spot was a few miles away from the cabin, so it was enough privacy to fool around without getting caught. When they were teens, Rae used to cover for him, saying he was near the lake.

What was Kenan up to? Was this pick on Rae day?

"This tree is wide and tall, very old. If you stand on its stump and hold on, leaning against the bark, if it's pretty windy, the tree will vibrate. Like. It's. Having. An. Orgasm," Kenan explained.

Brady grinned from ear to ear. "Sign me up."

This hour would take forever if her company kept these antics up, Rae thought. The other vehicle ran much smoother, so much quieter. Tobey had kept his eyes on the road, barely speaking two words the entire time. Marissa and Adam had sat way in the back to not be disturbed. She only heard slurping from their make-out session. Logan had been in the passenger seat while Rae enjoyed the middle all to herself. How nice that was. She could stretch her feet and look out the window in peace.

To tune out the kissing noises, she and Logan had participated in light conversation. She really enjoyed his company. Since he was respectful and sincere, it allowed Rae to feel comfortable enough to come out of her shell a little. She had wished she were kissing Logan. She felt like a high-schooler developing feelings on a forbidden student aide teacher.

Rae knew Kenan would never go for his sister dating his roommate.

The peace and quiet in the other Jeep gave her time to collect her thoughts. To ponder. Rae was traveling to a place where she swore she'd never return. A place that changed her life forever. She was on an emotional rollercoaster and needed time to process everything even if it'd be an in and out situation.

How could Kenan remain calm, in a joking mood? He had to be hurting just as much as her. Maybe he was better at hiding his emotions.

"JEALOUS MUCH?" MARISSA stuck her tongue out at Brady in the chips aisle of the convenience store. It was their last pit stop before reaching the cabin.

"Jealous?" Brady shrugged.

Marissa smirked. Naomi had told her how he couldn't keep her name out of his mouth in the other Jeep. He hated on Adam hardcore, sounded like Jealousy 101. Marissa's suspicions were confirmed when Naomi revealed that those words officially came out of Brady's mouth.

He had said, "I have a crush on Marissa. Tell me what I can do to win her heart." Music to her ears, but she couldn't let him know that. She couldn't let Brady have the upper hand of her feelings. That's why she always picked on him. Marissa couldn't let her guard down unless he made a move first.

She knew if she gave flirty, romantic attention to a random guy, Brady would come crawling. Guys hated not being center of attention, she laughed to herself. Marissa didn't know that her plan would work this fast, but she appreciated that it did. If Brady played his cards right, for the next three days, he'd get laid.

Adam had seemed uncomfortable and not thrilled by the news in the vehicle. That's how the cookie crumbled sometimes. They were not in a committed relationship—they literally just met. And what was up with his behavior in the parking lot? With Marissa's luck, of course, she snagged a jerk.

Oh well, he was only good for one thing, wouldn't need any talking involved. Besides, if Adam showed off, there were eight against one. Not good odds for him. If he was a major douche bag, he better contain it a little bit.

Brady was playing hardball. That's okay; she could wait. "I see how it is...Adam and I should win cutest couple. Do you have a camera to take pictures? I'd love to make a scrapbook for our vacation, the very first time with my future husband." Marissa wanted to lay it on thick. She had to make him think he had no shot in hell. It'd make him desire her even more.

It was time to put Brady on an emotional rollercoaster just as he'd put her through these past two months.

He rolled his eyes. "Good luck with that."

His jealous tone was sexy. Marissa waited for a flirty reply, but none came. No 'I thought I was your future husband'; no 'We can take pictures, but it wouldn't be appropriate for a scrapbook'; no wink, wink.

Brady seemed like he was in inner-turmoil or something, as if something was holding him back. What was it? Maybe he was hurt by her new *love interest*. To see him in a vulnerable state would be awesome, Marissa thought. All Brady had to do was pour his heart out to her, and she'd melt in his arms, forgetting about her new *boytoy*. Who in the hell was this Adam anyway?

Brady reached for Doritos.

"Ew, stinky breath."

"These are for Rae, her favorite chips."

"My favorite chips are...*Lays classic*," she said, licking her lips and hoping he would catch the pun.

"You should buy yourself some then." Brady smirked and walked away. Marissa pouted, fuming from ear to ear. She folded her arms across her chest. To her surprise, he peeked his head around the shelf to produce the sexiest grin ever. "Put your chips on the counter, and I'll pay for them."

"You just made my day." Marissa rolled her eyes. "What would I do without you, Brady?"

He stuck his tongue out and left again. Her knees buckled; she almost fell into the pile of chips on the shelf. Her stomach did back flips with excitement.

When would Brady stop being so stubborn and tell Marissa how he really felt? Maybe this weekend?

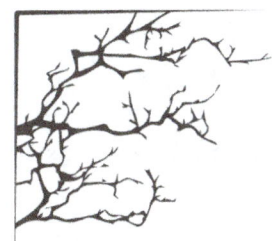

# Chapter Five

Rae paced back and forth in the parking lot, her hands shoved in her pockets. She counted slowly to ten, took deep breaths, and concentrated on a turtle moseying near the road. But no matter what she did, her heartbeat wouldn't stop accelerating. If she didn't calm down soon, she may die from a heart attack before even approaching the cabin.

If only...

Brady interrupted her thoughts as he approached her with a bag of Doritos in his hand. "These are for you."

A weak smile formed on Rae's lips. "Thanks."

"Are you okay?"

She sighed. "I need a drink."

"If you want a drinking partner, I'm all yours."

"Thanks, Brady, but I'll be okay."

"You sure?"

Rae nodded, afraid her voice would reveal her true emotions. They stood in silence for a little while, which was comforting to her.

"Hey, Rae and Brady, come mere for a second. We need to talk," Kenan said. They joined the group who stood by the Jeeps. Kenan frowned, glancing down at his cell phone. "I just got a phone call." He stared at his sister. "I'm sorry, Rae, but RL just said that he can't meet us until first thing in the morning. Something came up."

Sorry? Why would he be sorry? That was good news; now, they could head to the beach without all the drama beforehand. RL missed out by rescheduling. "You guys set up a new date? Maybe next month?" Yes in a month or two, maybe she could mentally prepare better.

Kenan and Tobey shared a look "We're meeting him in the morning like I just said."

Rae pouted and folded her arms across her chest. "Then we might as well drive to our hotel and reserve our rooms. We can hang out at the beach, then head back here early in the morning."

Kenan shook his head. "That's another three hours. We might as well stay at the cabin."

"I'm not staying there." She wiped a tear from her eye. "How can you even think to ask me that?"

Brady wrapped his arms around her while everyone else lowered their gazes to the ground. Kenan was the only one to keep steady eye contact with her. "Rae—"

"I'm not staying there, Kenan."

Naomi said, "Maybe driving to the hotel isn't such a bad idea. If you and Tobey are tired, then someone else can take over." She gave Rae a reassuring glance.

Tobey squeezed his girlfriend's waist, pulling her backwards into him. He was leaned over the hood of the vehicle. "Omi, it's not about being tired, it's about cost efficiency. Between all of us, we only have so much money for gas, food, and having a roof over our heads. Driving an additional six hours isn't in our budget."

*This can't be happening.* Rae's emotional rollercoaster was about to derail.

Marissa strode over to Rae and stood close beside her. "Maybe we can find a hotel around here."

Kenan smirked. "Good luck with that. Rae can tell you nothing is around here but this raggedy store. We're only forty-five minutes away from our vacation home. The only way to find a hotel would be to turn around, probably an hour ride tops. But good luck with that too. There's more than likely 'no vacant' signs. We're in a small town; trust me when I say we won't find a Comfort Suites or Holiday Inn in the mix."

Marissa put her hands on her hips. "We can at least try."

Kenan sighed, disheveling his hair. "What do you guys think?"

The only one not to speak up was Logan. He frowned during the majority of the conversation. Brady, Rae, and Marissa supported the idea of searching for a hotel. Naomi changed her tune after Tobey's rebuttal, causing her, Tobey, Selma, Adam, and Kenan against the idea.

Rae stared off into the distance with a lost, defeated expression. There was no point arguing. The most she could do was throw a temper tantrum and refuse to leave the parking lot, but Kenan would just drag her into the Jeep. Then her friends would think she was crazy. Actually, she needed to rethink her friendships. The only people who seemed to care about her were Brady and Marissa; everyone else would be on her shit list. Definitely Kenan for putting her in this position in the first place.

"There's a lake. We can hang out there for most of the night, then before we know it, it'll be morning. We'll sign the deed over to RL, then Rae and me can finally have closure." Kenan smiled at Rae. "You'd like that, wouldn't you? That was the whole point of doing this."

Rae stormed off. He sprinted after her. He grabbed her arm, but she yanked it away. "Get off of me!"

"I'm sorry, Rae."

"No, you're not. You could care less. I told you I didn't want to come, but you promised me we'd be in and out." She covered her mouth with her hand to hide her lips quivering. "I'll never forgive you for this, Kenan. Never."

He flinched.

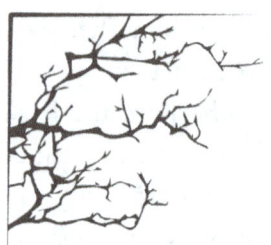

# Chapter Six

Kenan handed Selma the keys, so she led everyone, except him and Rae, into the cabin. He had pulled Rae away by the arm. She sat on the vehicle's hood, with her brother following her lead. He had wanted to make sure she was okay. He wasn't—he could break down and cry any minute—but he had to fake the funk; he had to be strong for his little sister.

The outside looked exactly the same. The same woods. The same grass. The same tall and thin trees. The same dirt paths. The same wooden cabin. There were no cracks or cobwebs. Nothing to indicate that the place had been abandoned ten years ago. Kenan believed the family in Virginia took care of the property. As far as he was concerned, after it was all said and done, anyone could take over for good. They could own it—burn it, chop it down, or live in it.

He wouldn't be around to care.

They sat in awkward silence, not knowing what to say to each other. Just being in the yard rushed back all the gruesome memories Kenan had tried to suppress. He could only imagine how it would feel to step inside the house, especially the living room where the nightmare happened. If he could've, he would've slain those intruders.

Unfortunately, his grandfather snuffed them on their way to trial right outside the courthouse. He had snapped, wanting revenge for them killing his baby girl. He didn't trust the justice system to convict the two males, who terrorized his family.

So, all at once, Rae and Kenan lost three family members. Their parents, they could never see again; their grandfather, they could only see behind a stained-glass window in prison.

Kenan looked over at Rae, who had a blank stare. What was she thinking about this very moment? She obviously hated his guts for talking her into coming here, but it was necessary. They needed closure, needed that final moment of peace before the end. Smiling, Kenan closed his eyes. He couldn't wait. He'd dreamt of it since the age of eighteen, Rae fifteen.

"Why are we doing this again?" she whispered.

He took a deep breath. "Because we're brave, and we can do it."

Rae nodded, only looking half convinced.

It was now or never to see if she recalled when they were teens. "Remember what we said in the attic?"

She wrinkled her nose and looked down to the ground. "Of course. No one forgets things like that." She frowned. "But we were young and depressed. We didn't mean it."

Kenan glanced at Rae, but she continued to lower her gaze. He squinted, reflecting on what she said. He had meant every word, and so did she. She shouldn't downplay it now. "Suicide letters don't have an expiration date."

Rae looked at him, then hurriedly looked away. She was wide-eyed with an open mouth expression. That was the ticket. Linger on that a bit. All actions had consequences, whether it was right away...or later.

WHEN RAE REACHED THE living room, it took all her willpower not to collapse on the wooden floor that had random rugs spread throughout. She shouldn't be there; it was too much. Too much drama. Too much heartache. She pouted, breaking into a sweat.

Marissa and Adam French kissed on the couch.

The couch. The spot where Rae and Kenan watched two men torture, gut, and slice their parents. The smell of blood and bile flooded her nostrils to the point she gagged. Her father's pleas for mercy and her mother's painful screams echoed once more through her brain. She immediately fled the room. When Rae ran into Logan in the hallway, the startling bump sent her flying backwards; she landed on her butt.

Logan took her by the hand to help her up. "Whoa, are you okay?"

Rae fought back tears and set foot into an empty bedroom. Not being able to control herself, she broke down and wept. Her body trembled; she couldn't get rid of the knot in her throat. Logan entered the room without knocking first. She didn't know if she could hold it together tonight. He slowly wrapped his arms around Rae as if he was afraid she was made out of glass and would break.

Even though Logan said nothing, just being there, he was very supportive. It meant everything to Rae that he let her cry on his shoulder. She tried to be silent, but it came out as loud wailing—sounding like a ghost shrieking through the house.

Marissa sprinted into the room. She stood beside Rae and gave her a hug from behind. "I'm so sorry, Rae."

A few moments passed, and Rae eventually composed herself; she wiped her eyes. She managed to squeak out a whisper, "I'm okay now. I promise."

Marissa said in a soothing voice, "Did something happen?" She furrowed an eyebrow. "We thought it'd be a good idea to leave you and Kenan outside for a while. Maybe it was too much to deal with, but you know you can always count on me. I'll be attached to your hip if you need me to be."

"No, enjoy yourself. That's why you guys came here." Rae shrugged her shoulders. "I guess it all hit me at once, and I wasn't prepared, but I'm fine now. Really."

Marissa and Logan looked like they had their doubts.

"I'LL ROOM WITH YOU," Marissa offered.

"Don't you want to room with Adam?" What was the point in bringing him here if she wasn't going to spend the night with him? Rae wondered.

Marissa looked at Logan. "Can you give us a minute?"

Logan nodded then left, probably waiting right outside the door. He had looked like he was agitated by her request.

Marissa whispered, "I don't care about Adam. I just brought him along to make someone jealous."

What? That was a lot of effort to make a guy jealous. Did she develop feelings for Kenan again? That would be weird, especially for him and Selma. Did Marissa have a crush on Tobey? That would start World War III—the wrath of

Naomi. Oh no, what if she had a crush on Logan? What if they liked the same guy?

Rae was too shy to make a move first; since Logan never had, she figured he only thought of her as a friend. Then again, they had deep and meaningful conversations where they could talk for hours and hours, so that had to mean something. Right?

Marissa was sexually aggressive. If she wanted a guy, it wasn't hard for her to put herself out there. It was already a pain being in Virginia; Rae didn't need any more heartache by watching her crush and best friend hit it off. Talk about a disappointment. Rae frowned. She would have no one to blame but herself, for not telling Logan how she felt, for not taking a chance.

Marissa was one of those people who shared a question with you that was intriguing, have you excited about hearing the answer, but then she would never reveal it. The more you'd ask, the easier it'd be for her to keep it to herself. She enjoyed having that mind power over others. Reverse psychology didn't work either. If you pretended not to care, it was easier for her to change the subject, so Rae knew better than to ask whom Marissa wanted to make jealous.

She reasoned it couldn't be Brady. Marissa wouldn't have to go to such lengths to get his attention. All she needed to say was, "Hey, wanna have sex?", and before she could blink her eyes, his pants would be off.

Rae hoped it wasn't Logan. Tobey was out of the question, so that left Kenan. Why didn't he ever tell her that his ex was hitting on him? No wonder Selma disliked Marissa. A girlfriend knew which women to watch around her man.

"Now this mystery will give your mind something else to occupy it with. You can thank me later," Marissa continued.

Rae smiled weakly. "Can't make the guy jealous if you sleep with me."

"Good point." Marissa held her hand, then wrapped her arm around her shoulder. "Are you sure you don't need me to stay with you?"

"Yeah, I'm fine."

"Well, if you need to talk, come knock on my door. I don't care how late it is."

"Thank you."

Marissa sighed. "I mean it, Rae."

"I will, Mar."

Marissa grinned. "Then again, if he thinks I'm bisexual, it may turn him on even more."

Rae shook her head, smacking her friend on the butt. "Try that mess with Naomi. Not me."

"Will you ever talk to her?"

"All she needs to do is apologize, then we can talk."

Marissa gave a never-going-to-happen look. Naomi was too self-centered to apologize by actually saying the words. Her pride wouldn't allow her to admit any wrongdoing, but if she truly cared about Rae, then she'd apologize in another way. By doing a nice gesture. Approaching her with small talk, making her breakfast, lunch, or dinner. Something.

Rae didn't want to stay a Negative Nancy and decided crying in the bedroom was exactly that. She figured it was time to leave, so they ended their conversation and left the room. As long as she'd stay in other areas, steering clear of the living room, she may be fine. Rae could enter and leave the cabin through the back exit connected to the kitchen. Easier said than done.

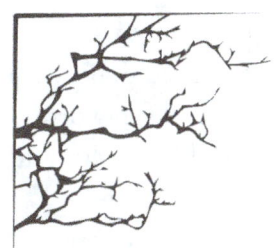

# Chapter Seven

Naomi felt an eerie sense being in Kenan and Rae's parents' master bedroom. She and Tobey had decided to take the biggest room to celebrate their two-year anniversary. It was lame sharing the special occasion with their friends, but her boyfriend had wanted to support Kenan. What about her? Besides this trip, which was already off course in the worst way possible, he had better buy an extravagant gift that she could cherish forever. A Tiffany bracelet. An engagement ring. A Coach bag. Diamond earrings. The list could go on and on till the end of time.

Naomi sat on the bed, shivering. Even though the air conditioner wasn't on, it was rather cold in the cabin, due to the electricity being off all this time. It would take a while for the generator to kick in. She was tempted to open a window to let in some heat.

Tobey put their clothes in a gigantic dresser that covered the entire bottom of the wall. With a three-day weekend, Naomi brought plenty of outfits; she planned to wear a different one for each activity. She brought about six outfits for each day—not including Friday—so that left eighteen ensembles total.

Besides, she didn't know how many times she'd have to wash. She didn't want to stink, smell like salt water, glisten from being out in the sun all day, or have sand lodged in areas even where her boyfriend couldn't reach. She also despised ticks and other bugs. Naomi planned to bathe quite a bit in case any fell on her. She never understood why the concept of a shower was so popular among people; she'd rather take a bubble bath because she deserved her beauty treatment.

Naomi had just washed herself. She hated the woods. She couldn't believe she let Tobey talk her into this. Wrapped in a towel, she rubbed lotion over her legs. She glanced over at him, hoping he'd be aroused. She sighed when he never looked up from his task.

How was Rae holding up? Naomi had witnessed her almost faint when she walked through the door, probably, no definitely, to cry. She wanted to be there for Rae, but assumed her presence would just make her best friend feel worse.

As if reading Naomi's mind, Tobey said, "Sweetie, you should sit down and talk with Rae. I know you miss her."

"How do you know?" Her ego tried to play it off, however, she did not sound convincing.

Tobey turned around with a seductive smile. "Because you haven't tried to jump my bones since you've been sitting there naked. It would've been a great opportunity to ask me to massage lotion all over your beautiful body."

Or he could've just offered, she thought. Would have been more romantic that way, but it didn't matter now; she was ready to get it on. Naomi stood up and let her towel fall on the wooden floor. Dust flew everywhere, kicking up mini-tornados. Tobey licked his lips while admiring her body.

She winked. "It's never too late. I'm sure I missed some spots."

"Well, then, I'd be more than happy to oblige," he quickly responded with a devilish smirk.

After their rendezvous, they both lay in bed under the purple satin sheets and a weird thought ran through Naomi's head. What if Kenan and Rae's parents' ghosts witnessed their lovemaking? Naomi could honestly say they put on a show.

Tobey ran his finger tantalizingly slow up and down her body. Naomi inhaled a breath of ecstasy and moaned his name. He grinned and kissed her belly. "We should probably go."

Way to rain on her parade. "Can't we just stay locked in this room all night? We'll socialize tomorrow." Naomi pouted.

"We shouldn't be rude," he rebutted and planted another kiss on her tummy, running his tongue up a slippery trail between her exposed breasts, up the side of her neck, past her chin, to the tip of her nose.

"You can't do things like that, turning me on, and expect me to want to leave."

"You'll be all right." He stood, grabbed her clothes off the dresser, and placed them on the bed beside her. "I'll meet you downstairs."

Naomi sighed. "Stay with me. It won't take long for me to get ready," she lied. She still needed to blow dry and flat iron her short haircut, reapply her make-up, all the while trying to put the clothes on without causing wrinkles. She was worth the wait though.

He grabbed the doorknob. "How do you expect me to behave myself when you're completely naked?" He placed his hand over his heart and left, shutting the door behind him.

BRADY AND LOGAN SAT on the porch in old, crusted rocking chairs. The two guys waited for everyone to join them outside. Logan couldn't believe Marissa had kicked him out of the room. It was unlikely that she and Rae would engage in women gossip, so why did a guy have to leave? He was offended. He could be trusted. If they brought up Rae's parents or something, then he could've handled it. Kenan probably already told him all the grueling details, so they didn't need to keep it a secret.

Logan already knew that Kenan and Rae were depressed; Kenan had confided in him. Instead of college, Kenan had moved in with his grandma, so he could start fresh and learn to breathe again in a new environment. He never stated he attended therapy sessions in North Carolina, but Logan always assumed that was part of the package deal.

Brady placed his hands behind his head. He didn't seem nervous at all. Would his mood change if he found out how Rae reacted earlier? Probably. Brady seemed to have a thing for her, but then again, he flirted with anything in a skirt and he would stick his penis in any willing girl.

They wore t-shirts, swimming trunks, and sandals. Brady even went as far as having orange, puffy floaties surrounding his arms since he couldn't swim. The plan was for everyone to head to the lake. Luckily, the sun was shining because Kenan had told them it was about a mile away. The last thing they needed was to get stuck in a storm.

Please no emergencies. Their cell phones didn't get service up there—at least Logan's didn't. He had the newest Sprint model; it wasn't like his phone or plan was cheap. Logan wondered if everyone else realized they were isolated from the outside world. Of course, Rae and Kenan knew, but did they warn anyone? They certainly hadn't told him, leaving Logan to enter the situation blindly.

He scanned the area and realized there were many hiding places for someone creepy to hide in the forest nestled in a valley. Logan grew up in the woods, so he knew how to navigate—his Boy Scout training came in handy. He knew how to set up a tent, obviously they weren't camping though. The Scouts also taught him how to start a fire without matches, catch fish with a stick, and how to follow the North Star and use the flow of the creek to seek civilization. Not only did he possess many skills; he also had instincts, and he knew that if someone were familiar with this area that they would strike at night. He was well aware that under the cover of darkness combined with the element of surprise, individuals meaning harm would be more successful.

Just in case, Logan should suggest keeping doors locked at all times, especially when no one was inside.

"Did Adam seem creepy to you in the Jeep?" Brady asked. Apparently, he had suspicions too. Minds tended to wander with no music, TV, or internet for distractions. Boredom could definitely play tricks on a person.

"Couldn't tell. Him and Marissa made out the entire time," Logan answered.

Brady smirked. "Of course, they did. Great, he'll gut us and leave her last."

Logan leaned up in his chair to be closer to him. He whispered, "Have some consideration. Don't say 'gutted.' Come on now."

"All I'm saying is I don't trust him, and I'm not sleeping here."

"Where are you going? It's not like there's a Holiday Inn nearby."

"Sleeping in the Jeep."

Logan laughed condescendingly. "Instead of relaxing in bed, you'd rather sleep upright in a car seat? Talk about uncomfortable."

"I brought my sleeping bag. When everyone gets their stuff out, then I can fold the back seats for more space. Enough room for me to lay down and even have a sleeping bag partner." Brady grinned. "I bet Rae would like to sleep with me instead of in the cabin."

Logan gave him a quick glance then looked away, trying to hide his impatience and jealousy. He could picture Brady convincing her to stay in the Jeep with him by bringing up the past as a way for her to agree. Then using Rae's vulnerability to have sex with her. She may be down, if private with no fear of someone hearing through the walls or seeing through the window. It'd get pitch dark at night, especially if no full moon.

Logan would have to stop this elaborate plan. Cock-block if you will.

"I see the wheels turning in your head. You got it bad for her, huh?" Brady smirked.

Logan figured it was best to shrug the comment off, to play it cool. "Rae's like a little sister to me."

Brady rose in his chair and leaned closer to him. "I know you're from West Virginia and all, but come on, the things you dream about doing to her isn't sibling related. At least say distant cousin or a step-sister."

Logan gulped. Brady was on to him, which was the last thing he needed. Brady was notorious for causing trouble. It was time to fight fire with fire. "If anyone has a crush on Rae, it's you."

"Nah, I'm not crushing. I graduated school a while ago. I have feelings for her. There's a difference."

Logan wished he could shout the truth from the rooftops, but too many consequences were involved. Even though he cherished every moment with Rae, he didn't know if she felt the same way. As if it would matter. He couldn't go there, although his heart wanted to. To add more insult to injury, Brady revealed that Kenan would approve of him dating Rae instead of Logan.

Brady must be lying. How could his roommate think that? Kenan would rather send Rae over to the womanizer instead of the sweet, romantic guy who would put his sister high up on a pedestal that she deserved. Kenan knew that Logan wasn't the type of guy to bring random girls home every night. He would be way more respectful than Brady could ever pretend to be.

If people wouldn't come outside soon, then Logan would go back into the kitchen to wait. He couldn't handle his temper being around this jackass any longer. How could Rae lower her standards and be friends with this creep?

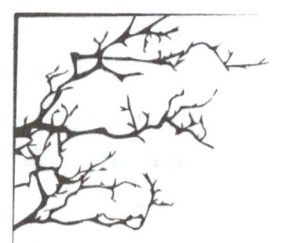

# Chapter Eight

The area could have been a perfect back setting to a summer camp horror movie where a psychopath terrorizes counselors and teens. Even the water offered itself where a group of friends could be attacked by sharks, piranhas, or any other Hollywood fabrication to boost high ratings and create a Blockbuster hit, Tobey thought.

There was an open field with low cut grass; obviously someone had mowed it recently. Random flowers and weeds blossomed through the ground. The water was clear blue so when people swam, they could see the bottom of the lake. At the back terrain, different size trees rose to the sky, inviting people to join the woods again.

Naomi tanned on a long, beach towel in the grass. She wore a pink bikini, leaving very little to the imagination, and she had worn a pink wrap dress on the hike to the lake. She swatted at random bugs flying in the air. Selma sat on Kenan's lap, while Tobey sat beside them with their feet dangling into the water—they were on the side of the dock. Rae sat on the bottom rung of the dock ladder. Farther out in the lake, Adam and Marissa kissed, while Logan and Brady stayed closer to land. They conversed with their friends who didn't get in the water. Brady kept teasing that he'd pull Rae into the lake. Even though she told him not to, it seemed like she was ready for it. That Rae was kind of disappointed that he hadn't done it yet. It was good that she seemed in a better mood, but then again...maybe she was just like her brother and was good at faking the funk.

Kenan hadn't exaggerated that this spot was about a mile or two away; the distance didn't bother Tobey or any of the other guys, except Brady. It hadn't bothered Rae either, but the other women nagged and complained. They weren't told to wear flip-flops. Hello, sticks; high, pokey grass; uprooted tree roots to accidentally trip over. What if they had to outrun a bear? Definitely couldn't do that in sandals or bare footed. And what if they needed to hide from a psychopath? The loud crunching sounds coming from their shoes would give away their location.

Tobey glanced over at Naomi, who listened to her iPod. He should go over and hang out with her. He missed her company; Tobey loved his girlfriend. Their friends joked that she was a handful, but not to him. He adored someone who challenged him and kept him on his toes.

"Woods is the perfect scene for horror movies," Brady said. He looked like a ten-year old in the public swimming pool—the one people didn't get near because there would be a yellow liquid ring around him resembling a force field, which kept his popularity to a bare minimum. Tobey really didn't think Brady had a chance with any of the women here, looking like an imbecile. Then again, maybe he could be trying the "help me act." Tobey wouldn't put it past him to try and scheme his way into a woman's heart.

"Nah, I think abandoned buildings, especially warehouses. They're always haunted," Tobey said.

"All I know is if I was in charge of my scary movie, the black people wouldn't die first." Kenan laughed.

Logan chuckled too as if sharing an inside joke among their ethnicity.

Brady raised an eyebrow. "Oh I see, so all the white people would die?"

Kenan smirked. "What you scared of, Brady? You're half Cherokee; that'll save you for a while."

"Would you have any of the black characters die?" Logan asked as if mentally noting if he'd be safe.

Kenan closed his eyes; he cracked his neck then looked at his friend. "No one would make it out alive."

Rae stood up quickly and climbed up the ladder to walk away. What were they thinking? Of course, she couldn't deal with that type of conversation. Tobey lowered his shoulders, flinching. Boys could be asinine sometimes; he knew because he was one.

"I'll go talk to her," Brady offered.

"No, give her space. She needs it," Kenan ordered.

No one said anything, causing awkward silence.

Eventually, Logan and Brady swam further out into the water, even Selma ended up going with them. They splashed each other while Selma tried to teach swimming lessons to Brady. What a sucker, Tobey laughed to himself.

He peeked back again; this time Naomi was missing. She had been so silent that he hadn't heard her leave. He assumed she went to check on Rae, which was the decent, friendly thing to do. Tobey would've followed Rae if Kenan hadn't suggested giving her space.

That left Tobey and Kenan alone on the dock. He couldn't believe Naomi disappeared without anyone acknowledging that fact. Weren't woods supposed to be loud when people walked through them? That was the whole point—no one should be able to sneak up on someone else. But apparently, they could be as quiet as a granny knitting a sweater with her hearing aide off.

Tobey rubbed his eyes. He prayed the girls wouldn't get lost.

"Do you think Naomi will apologize to Rae?" Kenan asked.

"Yeah. I told her that she should."

"Like she listens to you," he teased.

"She can't deny all this." Tobey held his hand up and down as if he was auctioning himself off as a prize.

Kenan laughed. "Please."

"Don't believe me, then why did we make love before heading here?"

Kenan frowned. "Ew, you two did it in my parents' room?"

"Sorry."

"It's not like they can use the room," he whispered, staring blankly off into space. "Besides, you should get it on as much as possible since you don't have much time left."

"Neither do you."

"A little more than you." They looked at each other in agreement. Thank goodness Tobey's best friend didn't hold a grudge about the hook-up situation. Now, Rae may be a different story.

Changing the subject, Kenan said, "I'm happy that Naomi and Rae will be able to make things right. I want Rae's time to be the best it can be under the circumstances, and Naomi should enjoy her time too. It's your anniversary after all."

Tobey nodded.

*CRACKLE. CRACKLE. SNAP. Snap.*

Who followed Rae? Quick, steady footsteps trailed behind her, but no one grabbed her attention by screaming her name or asking her to stop so they could catch up. In a panic, Rae strayed off sideways to lose her stalker. Before witnessing her parents' murders, she wouldn't have thought anything of it, but after that atrocious act, she knew anything horrendous could happen, especially if one was not prepared for it. The acres of land creeped her out. They hadn't even been here for more than three hours and she was ready to leave.

After picking up the thickest stick and biggest rock she could find, Rae ducked behind a tree and feared the worst. She was ready to use violence if need be. Sounds of footsteps came nearer. Nearer! She took a deep breath and gripped the stick with all her might. The stalker strolled past the tree. It was Naomi! Christ! She looked scared and lost while holding herself. Rae sighed, then quietly followed her on the path. She knew how to creep without making a sound because she once enjoyed many hunting seasons with her dad and brother.

Ten years ago, Rae and Kenan experienced the most horrible event possible. How could he joke about it? She had almost thrown up in disgust over their dreaded conversation at the lake. No consideration whatsoever.

Rae shadowed Naomi for a good couple of minutes, which she didn't notice. It'd definitely be easy to sneak up and attack her; Naomi better gain awareness if she wanted to survive the wilderness.

Rae hollered "Boo" to get her frenemy's attention. Naomi spun around. She seemed startled then relieved while tears fell from her eyes. She ran to Rae to give her a hug. "You have no idea how good it is to see you. I was scared that I was lost!"

Caught off guard, Rae wrapped her arms around Naomi. She could relate. The first time she got lost in the woods, she was ten. It had taken her parents two hours before they could find her. "What made you go off by yourself?"

"I wanted to check up on you. Are you all right?"

"Better than you at the moment." Rae smiled weakly.

They let go of each other.

"No seriously. Are you okay?" Naomi wiped a tear.

Rae took a deep breath. Why did Naomi act so caring? As if she'd actually support her.

It was more than watching their parents being brutally murdered in front of her and her brother. The two men took turns raping Rae and their mother. All the while, Kenan and their father, tied up, were forced to watch helplessly. No one should have to witness that. Their mom had whimpered barely above a whisper to remain strong for her family. However, Rae let out blood-curdling screams the entire time. She endured hours of so much pain due to the monsters' violent thrusts. They bruised and tore her virgin insides.

Rae tried so hard to forget, but she would always remember that she had lost her most precious possession to two older men who then killed their parents. Some things were meant to be kept secret, to be taken to the grave. No wonder Kenan was so overly protective of her.

Rae nodded. If she responded to Naomi's question, then they both would be crying. She kept her composure as best as she could.

"I'm sorry for everything," Naomi continued. She eyed Rae's weapons cautiously and took a step backward.

"No need to apologize out of fear." Rae tossed the rock and stick to the ground.

"I'm serious, Rae."

"I know. I just..." She sighed, fidgeting with her fingers. "I heard you," she whispered.

Naomi gulped. "What do you mean?"

"I heard you, Naomi." Rae frowned. "I know it's your anniversary, so I can understand why you don't want to be here. Heck, I don't want to be here either. But...I heard you joking with Tobey when you thought I couldn't hear." She paused. "You know what you said, and it hurt me deeply."

If she mentioned it to Tobey, then she would've ran her mouth to everyone and probably would've acted offended if they didn't laugh, Rae reasoned.

"Rae—"

"How could you say that you would never visit here with me because you'd be scared that I'd snap and kill all of you?"

"You know I didn't mean it, Rae. I was being stupid."

"That's an understatement."

Naomi pouted. "How can I make it up to you?"

Rae shook her head. "I honestly don't know."

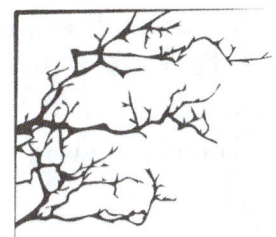

# Chapter Nine

People packed their towels, lotion, and wet clothes into book bags to leave the lake and return back to the cabin, but Marissa didn't want their lack of judgment to ruin her fun time. It was still bright outside. She wanted to continue playing in the water. "I'm not leaving yet," she announced to her friends. They stared at her as if she were crazy.

"Babe, we gotta stick with the group," Adam said.

Marissa drifted further into the lake. "What? You scared?"

"Not scared, just smart."

"Really? Because I don't remember you speaking up about us needing *food* before coming here."

Brady laughed. Marissa's face beamed with pride. She felt good when he got her sarcastic sense of humor.

Adam obviously wasn't amused. "You didn't either."

"Never claimed to be smart." She chuckled, joining the chorus of Brady's laughter.

"Adam's right. We shouldn't split up," Tobey said.

Kenan squeezed his shoulder. "Nah, it's okay. Let her stay if she wants." He focused his attention on Marissa. "Promise to stay here. Don't venture off anywhere. When we get back from the store, I'll walk over with a flashlight. I'm not kidding; it gets pitch dark out here, and there's no streetlights or anything. Please stay here, so you don't get lost."

Marissa smirked. "I promise."

"I mean it."

"I'll stay with her, Kenan, to keep her in check. Unless Adam wants to stay?" Brady offered.

Adam gave him an icy stare. "I'm going with the group."

Everyone turned to leave, but Kenan faced Marissa and Brady. "I'll be back as soon as I can."

He could take his time as far as she was concerned. She had Brady all to herself for at least one-hundred plus minutes, and she desired to please herself with every single one. She knew eventually that he would come to his senses. If he pretended to play hard to get, it wouldn't take long to reel him in. Brady was a horny dog after all.

Brady sat on the edge of the dock. "Trouble in paradise?"

"Ha. Ha. So original. Told you, you were jealous."

"Of A-dumb, please. He won't last past the three days."

"Really?" Marissa challenged.

"Yeah, I see the way you keep checking me out." He grinned seductively.

Marissa rolled her eyes. "A-dumb. I'd love to hear you say that to his face."

"No death wish today."

"Do you think he'd try to kill you if you hooked up with me?" It was time to put Brady to the test. He liked to dish it out, but could he take it. He could flirt non-stop with a woman past the uncomfortable stage and keep going. He was used to women ignoring or dissing him. Brady once said when dissed, that's an even bigger turn-on for him.

Marissa had yet to see how he reacted when the girl flirted back. He'd probably pee his pants or faint in surprise. If he'd act nervous, she'd eat him alive.

"Is that an invitation?" Brady asked.

"Hey, dumbass, what do you think?" Marissa swam to the dock and climbed up the ladder, splashing Brady with a little water. He eyed her up and down with desire while licking his lips.

She smiled as she dried off with a towel.

Marissa wasn't a prude by any means, but she didn't want to have sex with other people around. She knew the walls were thin in the cabin because she had heard Naomi and Tobey getting it on. Marissa was sure that Adam had heard it too. He fell silent, resembling a voyeur wanting to catch every moan escaping lovers' lips, every bed creak, and finally, the loud panting.

Brady scanned the area and then watched Marissa. "Why did you invite A-dumb in the first place? I don't trust him. He's sketchy. The douche lied when I asked him about his past. He's totally hiding something, but what? Has he revealed anything to you in between you sucking each others' tongues?"

She walked over to him, slowly dropping her towel to expose a red bikini. "Seriously, you want to talk about Adam at this moment? If I was alone with him, we'd be down to business by now. He'd have me all wet," she cooed.

Brady sighed. "I'm preoccupied, and it's your fault."

Marissa squatted down to face him sideways. He grinned. She looked down at the front of his swimming trunks and rubbed his package. He immediately popped an erection. "Is that for me?" she asked, while licking her lips.

"Marissa, I don't want a relationship."

"Don't worry, I won't be clingy," she promised. "Oh, and if you tell anyone, I'll deny it."

Once Brady lay on his back, Marissa pulled down his swimming trunks. He tried to get comfortable on the stiff wooden planks. She planned to please him to the point that he would feel like he was in a cozy, five-star bed, with silky sheets and fluffy pillows.

She proceeded to give him the best oral sex he ever had, while he massaged her scalp with his hands in a circular, slow, relaxing motion.

ROLLING HIS EYES, ADAM sighed. Maybe it was insensitive for him to leave Marissa like that. It didn't sit right that Brady had offered to stay. Did they scheme this since the beginning? If they thought they could play Adam for a fool, then they were sadly mistaken. He put in all the efforts of making out with Marissa, getting her in the mood, and he'd be damned if Brady got the full benefits of his hard work.

Putting girls in the mood was irksome, having to listen to them talk and talk about nothing interesting at all. Having to pretend to listen, so they don't get upset. Adam folded his arms across his chest and tapped his foot impatiently.

Adam, Tobey, Naomi, and Logan lined up by the front door in the living room. They waited on Kenan and Selma to return. Rae had stayed in the Jeep. Why did she have issues with this place? The cabin sitting in this picturesque forest was absolutely stunning.

Even though Adam came with Marissa, Selma was more of his type. He knew he couldn't get 'alone time' to work his magic because she seemed clingy and never left her boyfriend's side. The lucky bastard. That chick was hot!

Kenan and Selma entered the room; he placed the flashlight on the coffee table. "Okay, you guys ready?"

Adam took a step sideways to distance himself from the group. "Actually, I'm gonna stay here."

"But you were gung-ho on us all staying together. What made you change your mind?" Selma looked at him suspiciously. Hopefully, that joke in the parking lot wouldn't back fire on him.

"I feel sticky and yucky, so I want to take a shower. I trust that you guys will bring me back food," he lied. He planned to sneak off to the lake to spy on his jump-off and her dumbass friend.

"We can wait for you," Tobey offered.

"Nah, man. You know how cranky ladies get when they're hungry. PMSing. Heck, just breathing."

Selma's cheeks were red with anger. "Change your tone or get your own damn food."

Adam smirked. If he were in a bad mood, then he'd make sure to have his company in a bad mood too. If they all knew from the beginning that Adam would get played, then something would be in store for them.

To create peace, Kenan said, "We'll be back soon. Any food allergies or anything you refuse to eat?"

"Nah, I'm not picky."

"I'll stay with you." Tobey took a step towards the couch.

"No, come with us, baby." Naomi grabbed him by the arm. She sounded as though she thought Adam might corrupt her boring-ass boyfriend. A painting on its final leg to dry was less dull than Tobey was. "If you go through my stuff and steal anything, I'll personally hunt you down myself."

Adam chuckled. "Where could I go? You guys are stuck with me until Monday."

Finally, the group left. He didn't feel comfortable stepping outside until he heard both engines start and drive away. Adam grabbed the flashlight; he set out towards the lake. Like Hansel and Gretel, he left a trail of candy wrappers. He wasn't dumb enough to use real food. Wouldn't want to attract bears.

He stopped short when he came across Marissa and Brady in the near distance; he hid behind a tree, peeking his head to continue watching.

Marissa's legs were spread while Brady thrust inside her. He kissed her breasts and neck, never reaching her lips. They were naked on the dock. Adam could hear groaning in the distance.

How dare Brady get to her first! Adam better get his turn sometime tonight. Heck, he could probably walk right over there, pull down his swimming trunks, and take her from behind. Marissa was nothing but a slut, who was probably used to being sandwiched by two guys.

Adam should've known she was worthless. Who asks a stranger if they want a three-day hook-up? A prostitute, that's who. Brady saved him money because he was sure once they finished, she would demand to be paid. Who was her pimp? Probably all those guys.

Made sense, Adam reasoned. Each pimp assigned to a girl, and Brady was testing out his while Adam was supposed to be the willing client.

No wonder they all came to an isolated location. The crying temper tantrums were probably a part of role-playing. If Adam searched hard enough, he'd probably find hidden cameras in all the rooms. Heck, the bedrooms probably had regular video cameras set up, aimed at the bed. The girls didn't look filthy, so maybe they only occasionally dabbled in porn. Adam could get down with that—making a profit from this weekend.

But then again? Maybe Marissa wasn't a prostitute. Or porn star. Maybe she was just a cheating whore. The eyes didn't lie. Obsessed, Adam couldn't gaze away from his hook-up sexing someone else.

Fuck Brady. Fuck Marissa. And, most importantly, fuck their light source. Adam glanced down at the flashlight in his hands. It took all of him not to smash it against the tree he was leaning against; instead, he had a better idea. He'd hide it, so no one could use it. If they wanted to wander in the dark, oh well.

Actions had consequences. It just so happened that Marissa and Brady's vile behavior would affect the group in the worst way.

Adam spat on the ground, walking away. He needed to find a suitable hiding place, a place only he knew where it was. The flashlight would be useful to spy on people. He hoped Marissa and Brady would get lost in the woods, eventually starving or freezing to death. Or better yet, attacked by a bear. That would be a fair judgment for bruising his ego.

Not paying attention, Adam got lost. Somehow he must have went right instead of left, or left instead of right, because he thought he'd be at the cabin by now. He didn't think he was anywhere near. Adam came across a broke down building with rotten wood, the door hanging off the handle, and tall grass blocking the entranceway, daring trespassers to trek into tick territory.

This would be a great place to hide something, then reality hit Adam in the face. How would he get himself out of this lost predicament if he didn't have light himself? He cast an eye over the area. "Damn, why did I let that bitch talk me into entering *Wrong Turn* territory?"

His mind ran with fear. What if a crazy cannibal family lived nearby and planned to eat him? What if they wanted Hawaiian dark meat? Having good taste, he knew they'd find him delicious. Damn his attractive looks and clean hygiene. The one-tooth, three-eyed monster would probably kidnap Adam, force him to marry his five-breasted daughter with webfeet and half-formed ears with no upper lip. Yuck! What would their kids look like? Then again, they probably married inside the family. Those sick bastards!

Adam wished he had stayed with the group inside an air-conditioned Jeep. Not out in the boondocks to burn up. He sweated like a pig. Why didn't he stay at the cabin to take a shower?

Letting curiosity take over, he entered the shed. Why would Kenan lie and say neighbors weren't close by? Then whose shed was this? It had all new and shiny tools—hammers, slicers and dicers, axes—hanging on the wall for a masked or scarred psycho killer. Everything looked like it would be painful in an attack.

Someone was lying. Why?

Adam went back to his original plan of hiding the flashlight. He liked to think he had brain cells, so he should be able to find his way back to the cabin. He had left a trail of candy wrappers for a reason. Hopefully, there'd be a full moon tonight.

He searched for the perfect hiding place; he looked inside a huge cabinet. Once he opened it, he found a masonry jar containing Moonshine. Adam smiled and grabbed it. He took a sip, feeling warmth through his veins immediately. It probably wasn't wise to drink liquor without eating or drinking plenty of water first, but with the predicament Adam was in, he needed to get tipsy.

He chugged some more, not being cautious of slowing down. Free liquor was always the best. He sat on a narrow, red toolbox that he wiped off with an old pair of dungarees; no way was he sitting on the dusty floor.

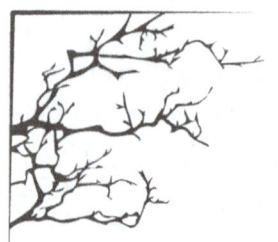

# Chapter Ten

Where's the flashlight? Kenan recalled setting it down on the coffee table. The damned thing did not grow legs and march itself out of the room. He rolled his eyes. All during the trip, he had to hear everyone say they didn't trust Adam, questioning Kenan why he let him stay in the cabin alone.

What could Kenan have done? It's not as if this weekend was a dictatorship where he'd coerce everyone into submission. Was he supposed to knock Adam over the head and drag him into the Jeep? Or was he supposed to bribe him with doggy biscuits?

Kenan looked at Naomi; of course, she had to put in her two cents. "Told you he couldn't be trusted. He's probably long gone with all our stuff." She darted upstairs.

He shook his head. How could Adam carry it all, genius?

Naomi came back to the first floor. "All our stuff is still here, but Adam's gone." Wide-eyed, she continued, "With our flashlight!"

"Don't worry. There's two more." Kenan found the other flashlights in the same location as the first one. He tried to turn them on, but they wouldn't work.

Naomi pouted. "Great. No batteries. We were just at the store."

"You act like there's no double AA batteries around." Selma came to her boyfriend's rescue.

Naomi crossed her arms over her chest. As if that wasn't enough, she then put her hands on her hips. "Well, are there?"

Kenan shared a look with Rae. He had no idea, but he was leaning toward the answer of no. "Listen, Adam probably went back to the lake to hang out with Brady and Marissa. You guys put the food away, and I'll go get them."

"Not by yourself?" Logan asked.

"I need to make things right. Trust me. I know these woods like the back of my hand."

Selma pouted, grabbing Kenan's hand and leading him outside to the porch. All he noticed was her shadowy figure, then his eyes adjusted to the dark. "I don't want you to go by yourself. You could get hurt."

"I'll be fine."

"Baby, I don't want you to go."

"Sel, I promised them. Am I supposed to leave Mar and Brady out there all night?"

"Mar?"

"What?"

"You called her Mar," Selma said in an accusatory tone. "I don't want you alone with her!"

"How am I alone if Adam and Brady are with me?" Kenan grabbed her hand and kissed it. "Stop acting jealous. You don't have to be. I'm with you, Sel, and I'm not looking for anyone else." He held her in his arms and kissed her on top of the head.

Her body relaxed. "I'll go with you."

Kenan wasn't really in the mood to keep track of someone else on the journey as well as having to look out for himself. Besides, he didn't trust that Selma wouldn't instigate something with Marissa, and his ex didn't deserve that. "Stay with Rae."

"Why? She doesn't even like me."

"What? Yeah she does."

"Well, she has a funny way of showing it."

"You know Rae is quiet." He tapped his foot impatiently. "That's just her nature, doesn't mean she doesn't like you."

"I bet Marissa dissed me in front of Naomi and Rae. That's probably why they never gave me a chance."

Kenan sighed and put on his hoodie. "Sel, we'll talk later, but I really should go get them. It'll be freezing soon."

"Whatever." She turned to walk away, but Kenan grabbed her hand. She yelled, "What?"

"I love you."

"I love you too," Selma's voice softened.

Kenan hoped for the best while hiking the trail from earlier. What if they didn't listen and went off somewhere? How in the hell was he supposed to find them now, without a flashlight? And why didn't he ask another guy to tag along?

Deep down, he knew the answer to the last question. He hoped to get Marissa alone, to get inside her head for a bit. He thought it'd be best if they got closure, then he wouldn't get caught calling his ex by a pet name—Mar really? Did he really utter that in front of his girlfriend? What a slip-up in the worst way.

STANDING AGAINST A tree, Kenan spotted Marissa and Brady's shadows at a distance. The moon and stars illuminated the open area. Tall trees didn't block the natural light.

At least, they were smart enough to get out of the water to have time to dry off, but where the hell was Adam? Kenan definitely only caught a glimpse of two bodies. Maybe Adam brought them the flashlight and then walked back to the cabin? They would've crossed paths. Right?

Kenan stopped spying; he headed towards the lake.

Brady stood up from the dock. "Hey, stranger."

"You guys missed me?"

"Not that much." Brady grinned.

Kenan browsed the area. "Where's Adam?"

"I thought he was with you," Marissa said.

"No, when we got back, he said he was staying to clean up, but he wasn't there when we got back from the store. And the flashlight's gone. I assumed he came back here to hang out with you guys again."

"We never saw him." Marissa interweaved her fingers nervously. "Do you think something happened to him?"

"Nah." Adam was a big boy; he should be all right. If not, he should've listened. No, Kenan couldn't justify him getting hurt. "I didn't pass him, so—"

"Wait. A-dumb did mention that he liked hiking in Colorado. That's probably what he's doing...I'm hungry. Can we head back now since you didn't bring food with you?" Brady asked.

"Yeah let's go."

Marissa remained seated. "I'm not ready yet."

"Are you serious?" Brady asked.

"Yes. I love the view, and I want to stay here."

Brady sighed. "It's not like we can't come back tomorrow."

"You guys can go."

"And leave you by yourself. Hell no," Kenan said firmly.

"What if Adam's plotting against us? I mean, maybe he hiked back but saw something to make him mad. Now, he wants to kill me and Marissa."

Kenan scratched his head, raising his brow. "What?"

"Hypothetically speaking." Brady was a drama king, who always made a mountain out of a molehill. He would not let go of the theory that Adam, the stranger, couldn't be trusted.

Kenan wished he'd give it a rest already. "Tell you what, if that happens, then I got your back."

Out of nowhere, a glow flashed in the distance. Tobey appeared out of the shadows.

"Did you find Adam?" Kenan asked.

"He's still missing?" Tobey counter-questioned.

"I'll find him; he can sweat a little since he didn't listen."

"We found batteries, so the flashlights work...I came to get you."

Brady moved closer to Tobey. "Great. I can't wait to eat."

"You guys coming?" Tobey asked.

"Yeah," Kenan answered.

Marissa grabbed his hand, causing him to look down in her direction. "Stay with me, just a little while longer."

They were not exactly on a picnic or in an amusement park. They were in the woods where hunters set animal traps. Bears roamed around. Anything could happen, and Marissa wanted to hang around all willy-nilly. However, Kenan never could say no to a pretty face. "We'll go back to the cabin later. First, we'll look for Adam; you two go ahead."

"But what about the light?" Brady asked as if there was no way Kenan and Marissa would take hold of the flashlight.

"We'll be fine. I know my way around these parts." Kenan looked at Marissa. "Do you trust me?"

She nodded. "Of course."

The boys left because they had common sense. Kenan sighed. "You're gonna get me in trouble with Selma."

Marissa locked arms with him. "She'll have to get over it. If she allowed us to spend time together, then I wouldn't have to scheme."

He smiled. They conversed for a while; if he had a watch, he could tell that an hour or two passed. Time seemed to stand still when he was around his ex. Eventually, they shared silence until he broke the ice. "I need to confess something to you."

"What?"

Kenan took a deep breath. "I didn't spend time with Grandma those few years I was away. I was in a psych ward; that's why I wasn't mad that you moved on without me. I felt that I didn't deserve you. You could do better."

Marissa covered her mouth. "What?"

"You can't tell Rae. She doesn't know, and I want to keep it that way."

"Are you pulling my chain?"

He remained silent, studying her silhouette. He could sense the wheels turning in her head. He began laughing.

"That's not funny. Why didn't you tell me? I could've been there for you."

"How sweet, but I was just playing."

Marissa hit his arm. "That's just cruel."

"Its payback for making me stay behind with you; plus, you couldn't keep your guy in check."

"Adam is not my guy." She rolled her eyes.

Kenan chuckled to himself. Only Marissa would get tired of a guy in less than five hours. "You don't have to lie; I'm not jealous."

"I'm jealous of Selma. She says 'jump,' and you ask 'how high,'" Marissa whined. "She's really trying to ruin our friendship."

He had refused to let Selma badmouth Marissa, so he wouldn't let Marissa diss Selma either. Both girls were in his heart. They'd just have to accept that. The exes were still bonding until they were interrupted by someone approaching them with a flashlight.

"Hey," the person said.

"Hey, stranger." Kenan smiled. "I'm leaving, so you better come on, girl."

"Or you can stay with me."

"I'd like that." Marissa grinned to the person. Kenan strolled away.

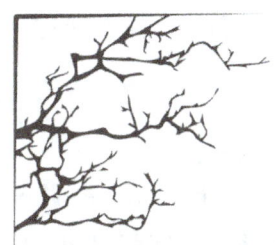

# Chapter Eleven

Brady's back ached. It was stuffy inside the small space, so he rolled down a window. Who knew how many mosquitoes would bite him. Maybe he should've rethought the whole sleeping in the vehicle idea.

He tossed and turned in his camouflage sleeping bag meant for two. A-dumb hadn't gone to the store; did he walk back to the lake and witness them hooking up? If so, Brady was definitely on A-dumb's hit list. Was Marissa hooking up with Kenan right now? It'd be beneficial for someone else to have the stranger's hatred too.

When Brady heard a knock on the window, he shifted his body to take a peek at his visitor. He was shocked that it was Rae—well her shadowy figure. She was the only one with a wavy afro. He unlocked the Jeep door, letting her in. "Hey, what are you doing here?"

He couldn't believe Rae was here, even if only just to say goodnight. The fact that she thought he was special enough to think of before going to bed would always be a plus in his book.

"Want me to leave?" she asked.

"Hell no, girl." Brady closed the door and locked it, emphasizing how much he desired her to stay.

Rae smiled, blushing. "Were you asleep?"

"No, I was thinking about you."

She was beautiful when she acted shy and nervous. Why did he blow it by hooking up with Marissa? Hopefully, she wouldn't spill the beans because their clique was the type not wanting to date their friend's ex—sloppy seconds. Brady should've had more self-control. If he would had known Rae would come to him by the end of the night, then he would have never jeopardized anything.

Rae placed a strand of hair behind her ear. "So you won't mind my company? Logan told me where you were when I checked in your room to say goodnight. I couldn't sleep and thought maybe I could if I came out here to sleep with you."

A wide grin formed on Brady's lips.

"You know what I mean, to sleep *next* to you, not *with* you."

He laughed. She was the cutest thing clarifying things for him; he read between the lines, but was grateful that he won over Logan and Kenan. For the night, Rae trusted Brady. He wouldn't let her down.

Since she didn't bring her own covers or sheets, she was inviting herself to lie in his sleeping bag. No more games. Brady wouldn't crack jokes or act unaffected by this. He was touched by this moment, his heart skipping a beat. Maybe it was time to see how Rae felt about him. To see if she'd make a move like rubbing her leg against his, asking him to hold her. Maybe saying she's cold and asking Brady to wear his sweatshirt.

Dang it. Why didn't he bring his sweatshirt after taking a shower? He wore a black long sleeve shirt and gray sweats.

Rae leaned up against the car's interior door, resting her back and sitting her legs up to wrap her arms around them. She placed her head on top of her knees. "Thanks for letting me stay with you. It means a lot."

"Well, how you're sitting, it seems like you're just here to visit instead of stay."

"What do you mean?" She looked curious.

"Someone who wants to stay would lay down beside me and get comfy. Instead you're by the door like you could leave at any moment, like maybe you're regretting coming down here." Brady was a history major, but his real passion was psychology. Well, psychology and music.

Rae smiled and moved closer to Brady. "I don't regret being here." He unzipped his sleeping bag, so she could get in. Why did he get a gigantic one? He should've brought a smaller one, so he'd have an excuse to cuddle with her. Rae zipped the sleeping bag up and turned to face Brady; she lay on her stomach with her head resting on her arms. "Who would've thought a car floor would be roomy and cozy."

"I know, right?" Brady wiped sweat from his forehead. She wouldn't take her eyes off of him; that was his MO.

They engaged in small talk. He didn't know about Rae, but he was spent. She asked him to sing her a bedtime song, which brought up the topic that he wanted to audition for *The Voice*. Ever since the first season, Brady knew he was destined to be on the show, gain fans and popularity, then become so famous that people bought tickets to his sold-out concerts.

That's why he had been disappointed that he forgot his guitar; he could've been practicing. He sang Civil Twilight's "Letters from the sky." Like predicted, she was captivated.

"Someone will definitely turn around for you." Rae grinned. "All four actually."

"Hopefully Adam Levine. He's the type of music career I want."

She drifted off to sleep. Even though he was tired, he listened to her snore softly. He couldn't take his eyes off of her no matter how much he tried. She was there with him; that's all that mattered. If Rae asked to spend every night with Brady on their vacation, then it would be the luckiest trip ever. Could dreams really come true?

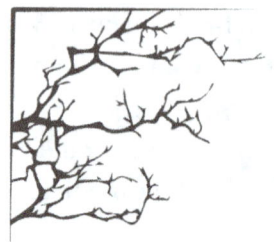

# Chapter Twelve

The sun beat down on Tobey while he banged on the Jeep's window in case Brady and Rae were sound sleepers. They jolted awake in total confusion. He wondered if they did anything last night. Any idiot with half a brain could tell that Brady had feelings for Rae. Last night he had gotten his wish of spending the night with her.

Did Brady spend his time wisely, focusing on the long term? Or did he think with his penis, messing up a great friendship? Tobey hoped he didn't do anything stupid. Rae didn't need any extra stress put on her.

Groggily, Brady opened the door; he rubbed his eyes. "Hey man, what was that for?"

Tobey couldn't believe he let his mind get distracted; they had an emergency on their hands. "Have you seen Marissa or Adam?"

Brady looked inside the Jeep. "Where would they fit?"

"Wait. Are they missing?" Rae asked in a panic.

"I don't know. I mean they aren't in their rooms. Everyone thought we heard them come in last night before going to bed, but now we're not sure. I mean their bed is completely made up, suitcases not touched."

Brady rolled his eyes. "Aren't we good hosts?"

"Now isn't the time for jokes," Rae said.

"Sorry." Brady put his head down as if ashamed. So whipped.

They went inside and found Logan, Kenan, Selma, and Naomi sitting around the rectangular wooden kitchen table, enjoying their morning cup of coffee. "Have you guys seen Marissa or Adam?" Selma asked.

Brady and Rae shook their heads in unison.

"Well, the ladies can stay here to see if they come back, and the guys can go out and look for them. It'll be more effective if we split up in the woods," Kenan suggested.

"You want me to go too?" Brady asked.

"You're a guy, aren't you?" Logan said bitterly.

"It'd be better if a guy stays with the girls. What if they need help?" Brady ignored Logan, focusing his attention on the group.

Selma folded her arms across her plaid tank top. "We can take care of ourselves."

"Can't you help a guy out?"

"Think less about you, Brady, and more on the task at hand." Selma took a sip of coffee.

He rolled his eyes. "Oh, please, I'm sure they're at the lake making out and having a grand ole time while everyone else gets woken up from a peaceful sleep."

Tobey hoped he wouldn't be teamed up with Brady because he probably wouldn't stop griping the entire time. But Tobey was too much of a nice guy to speak up, so that's exactly what would happen. He sighed.

"Hopefully, you're right," Naomi said.

"I mean seriously. We don't need chaperones; we're old enough to take care of ourselves." Brady looked at Kenan. "What do you think happened to them?"

Everyone observed Rae in silence, which caused Brady to glance at her too. She frowned. Brady could be clueless sometimes. Of course, no one could say they thought Marissa and Adam were dead somewhere, insinuating that this vicinity was cursed. They couldn't afford to upset Rae.

NAOMI, DRESSED IN AN off-shoulder purple top and black spandex shorts, looked out the window in the living room. There were no blinds or anything to cover the stained glass. It had been a while, and the guys still weren't back. She wondered how much ground they had to cover. She hoped that Marissa and Adam were okay. Brady was right—the missing couple were making out at the lake. An early rendezvous. Something she and Tobey should be doing to celebrate.

And people said Naomi was an inconsiderate friend. Please. Marissa topped the cake, bringing a complete stranger with them, when no one knew him at all or trusted him. Then the douche bag had the audacity to say he was crazy.

What if Adam hurt Marissa, and they weren't being inconsiderate buffoons by not telling anyone they were leaving?

Selma stood in front of the window with her hands in her blue, baggy, boyfriend style jean's pockets. Who was she to speak for all the women and say they could take care of themselves? Hopefully, nothing zany happened last night. But what if it did? What if killers or robbers busted through the door? Was Selma supposed to save them by giving the bad guys her famous aloof stare?

A guy should've stayed at the cabin too. It'd be valuable for someone to stay and fight.

Naomi finally noticed that Rae had never joined them in the living room. Oh no, not another one missing. She decided to go search for her friend. She walked away without telling Selma where she was going. Selma seemed so distracted that she hadn't even acknowledged Naomi leaving.

She discovered Rae sitting at the top of the stairs. Rae looked discouraged, so she gave her a hug before sitting closely beside her. "The guys will find them unharmed, then we all can laugh about this later." Naomi patted her friend's knee.

"You can't promise that. There are bears out there. Oh my gosh, what if Marissa never got out of the water and froze to death?"

"Highly unlikely."

"But there's a possibility." Rae fidgeted with her hands, avoiding eye contact with Naomi. "I saw how everyone looked at me in the kitchen. I can't go through any more brutal attacks. I can't."

Naomi grabbed Rae's hand. "You won't have to."

"You can't promise that." Rae pouted.

Naomi realized there was no comforting her at the moment. Whatever she said probably made Rae feel worse, so for once in Naomi's life, she decided to sit in silence with her best friend.

Suddenly, Selma, uninvited, joined them on the steps. She didn't bother giving any words of encouragement or small talk to break the ice. Why did she come over then? Naomi laughed to herself, surprised Selma hadn't demanded to go search with her one and only, Kenan.

Selma glared at Naomi with squinty eyes. "She's your friend. Next time put her in check and tell her she needs to keep everyone updated on where she's going. I can think of a better way to spend my morning."

"Don't talk bad about Marissa." Rae balled her hand into a fist. "Not now."

"What? It's not like anything's wrong. She'll come strutting in here without an apology. She'll blame us for overreacting because she's unappreciative of friends."

"Selma, not now!"

She looked at Rae gobsmacked.

Rae whispered, "Something's happened. I can feel it."

"How?" Naomi asked.

"It's the same feeling I had right before the robbers broke in."

"Your mind is playing tricks on you because of what you experienced here, pretty understandable," Selma said.

"It's not in my head; I feel it." Rae turned to Naomi with pleading eyes. "I feel it."

"It's okay, Rae. I believe you." Naomi wrapped her arm around her friend. "Just drop it, Selma. Why don't you go back to the window and check on the guys?"

"No way they're back now. They've only been gone for about ten minutes," Selma said.

It's only been that long? It seemed like an eternity. "Then you can boil some water?"

"No one's pregnant," Selma snapped back. Why couldn't she get the hint to leave them alone in peace?

Hopefully, their back and forth was distracting Rae from her crazy, disturbed thoughts. If she didn't watch out, someone may force her into a psych ward. "Then look for a first-aid kit."

"Why? Kenan will know where it is. Or she will." Selma looked at Rae. "Do you remember where it is?"

Naomi rolled her eyes. She hated that Selma didn't jump on her command. How could she uphold Queen Bee status if an opposer in the group didn't listen, rather questioned everything?

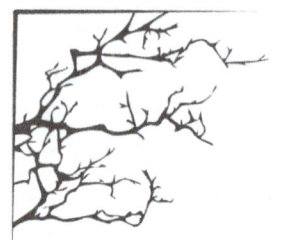

# Chapter Thirteen

Logan and Kenan canvassed a part of the woods while Tobey and Brady searched the area that had thicker branched trees and dirt paths. Brady couldn't believe this was happening right now. He could've woken up to the sight of Rae, who looked effortless in the morning. They could've locked in a gaze, then had a morning kiss. Or she could've woken up in his arms. He'd know if he had crossed a line if Rae smiled or not. Now, that dream was shot to hell because attention seekers wanted to show off. People fell right into Marissa and Adam's trap.

And it's not as if Brady was salty because he was jealous of Marissa and Adam hooking up after they did. It was the principle of the matter. At least don't take A-dumb to the same spot they had sex, switch that up a little bit. "I still don't see what the big deal is."

"We want to make sure nothing bad has happened," Tobey said.

"But they're grown folks. I mean, say I woke up at the butt crack of dawn to go for a jog. I wouldn't necessarily wake anyone up to tell them that."

"But wouldn't you leave a note?"

Brady was at a loss for words; he would, he guessed. That would make sense, so people would know what direction to focus on if he got lost, fainted from lack of water, or sprained an ankle by tripping on a tree stump. Now, everyone's rationalization made sense of why they were worried.

If they would have pointed that out to Brady in the first place, then he would had understood sooner and not looked like a jackass in front of Rae.

To save face that he may be wrong—he was but would never admit it to anyone else—Brady said, "I don't know. I'll think about it and get back to you."

Tobey cracked his neck. "I'll be waiting."

Brady smirked. "Am I ruining your *perfect* anniversary?"

"Not at all."

Brady scanned the area; he didn't see anything useful to pinpoint where Marissa and A-dumb could be.

Tobey threw his arm out to stop Brady from walking. "Look over there."

He turned, focusing on where Tobey pointed his finger. A broke down shed with the door cracked open was in plain view. Why did Brady let his friends talk him into coming on this vacation again? Wait, they never even invited him. He had to invite himself. He guessed his only friend was Rae. It was things like this Brady decided to brood over before meeting his untimely death. Who knew what or who was in that building?

Brady frowned. "Let me guess, you wanna look in there?"

Tobey smiled, patting him on the shoulder. "Come on."

Like a lapdog, he followed orders by following Tobey into the abandoned building. Nothing but tools and weapons hung from the walls and ceiling. This was not good. Brady could admit he wasn't the type of dude to know about assembling or fixing things, so maybe he was overreacting when seeing all these objects. Maybe they were all necessary to have. A *big* maybe.

Brady stood by the door, too nervous to step any further into the kill dungeon. "They're not here. Let's go, dude."

Tobey continued to slide his feet on the concrete floor, blowing dust balls as he glided his hands over the tools. "Someone's been here recently."

"How can you tell?"

"I smell stale cologne. Plus, someone opened this Moonshine and almost chugged it all."

The guys shared a look. "Maybe Adam and Marissa were in here," Brady guessed.

Maybe they got lost and went for the nearest shelter, found some booze, got drunk, and did the smart thing by leaving this creepy place. There was no rule saying you couldn't get drunk or high in the morning, Brady reasoned.

"What if this is someone else's shed? Maybe he didn't like trespassers and wanted to teach the outsiders a lesson." It seemed like Tobey watched too many horror movies.

"WHERE DO YOU THINK they are?" Logan asked.

Kenan sat on top of a rotted tree stump. He rubbed his forehead. "I have no idea. If I did, we'd already be there."

Logan sighed. He had no choice but to follow Kenan's lead because he knew the area more than Logan did.

He wanted to ask Kenan a more personal question, like did he think something awful happened to them? Kenan was quiet during their search and had calmly taken over this morning that Logan couldn't tell if his friend was freaking out.

If a tragedy happened ten years ago, it could occur again.

The boys didn't speak for a while. Logan tapped his sneaker between the moss and tall grass. They should be trying to pinpoint their friends' whereabouts. What was Kenan doing? Every second counted. "I'm sorry. I know it must be hard for you."

"What?"

Logan lowered his eyes to the ground, whispering, "Being here at the cabin."

"I slept like a baby last night, actually."

"Well, Rae was having a hard time. Last night she came to me and said she couldn't sleep. She asked where Brady was."

"Why didn't she come to me?" Kenan frowned, standing up.

Logan shrugged his shoulders.

He rubbed his forehead and sighed. "Why didn't you tell me? You could've woken me up if I was asleep."

"The thought didn't even cross my mind."

"Well, next time it should." Kenan cracked his neck. "I'm sorry. I'm just worried about her. It's like she's afraid to bring up the past because she's trying to protect me."

"Just like you're trying to protect her."

"She must be really freaking out this morning. I should've stayed with her." Kenan threw on his black hoodie because a light drizzle started. Logan wished he would have brought something to protect himself from the rain, while hoping it wouldn't storm. He wore a red t-shirt and red athletic shorts that went past his knees. Even though he wasn't afraid of thunder and lightning, Logan was smart. There would be no protection with only trees surrounding them.

No one could afford to get hurt at this place. Who knew how far the hospital was.

"I can't think of any place to cover that Brady and Tobey won't reach in their search, so let's just head to the lake. We need to get back as soon as possible because *I'm* the only one who can calm Rae down," Kenan continued.

They began walking again.

Kenan was wrong, Logan thought. He wasn't the only one who could calm his sister down. Logan did a fine job last night; that's why it pained him that she ran to Brady. He was a jerk. She'd rather cuddle with him instead of Logan. At least, Logan hoped that's all they did. He wanted to beat the crap out of Brady when they had entered the kitchen, wanted to smack that smug smirk right off his ugly face.

Kenan didn't seem to mind Rae being with Brady. What was up with that? Logan glanced over at his search buddy, who just strolled along. He felt bad that his mind was preoccupied; he could barely focus. It wasn't right because if Logan's friends worried about him, he'd want their full, undivided attention while searching for him. Not a half-ass attempt. Logan scolded himself, checking the right side of the foliage.

They reached the opening field of the lake. Adam was pulling a body out of the water. Kenan raced towards them. Logan sprinted too. Kenan's eyes widened while he helped Adam pull Marissa from the icy water. They lay her down in the grass. Logan covered his mouth; she was blue all over. Her face was frozen into an open mouth expression as if during her last few moments on Earth, she tried to scream "help."

Kenan fell to his knees and whispered, "Marissa." He placed his head on her chest to listen for a heartbeat. Then he did mouth to mouth resuscitation.

In a rage, Logan tackled Adam to the ground. Adam's breath smelled like ass, and he still wore the same clothes as yesterday. He didn't even fight back. His eyes were dark red, as though the devil was in him. What other reason could explain why he killed Marissa? Caught red-handed. "What the fuck did you do?"

"Get off of me!"

"I will fucking kill you!"

Kenan yanked Logan off of Adam, so Adam tried to crawl away. Kenan grabbed his shirt collar, almost choking him. He gagged while he fell on his back. Logan, with fists raised, tried to jump him again. Kenan stretched out his hands to stop him.

Adam flinched. "Keep him away from me!"

"What happened?" Kenan asked.

"Keep him away from me!" Adam repeated, looking at Logan.

Kenan slapped Adam in the face. "What happened? Answer me, or I'll let him do whatever he wants to you."

Adam held his hands in surrender. "I found her a little before you guys did. She was face down floating in the lake, so I was pulling her out when you guys arrived."

"You liar! You killed her!" Logan climbed over Kenan to get to Adam again. His dad used to beat on his mom all the time before she got the courage to leave him. Logan hated men who were violent towards women. If it were up to him, they'd all rot in hell.

Kenan shoved him. "Calm down, Logan."

Logan marched around in circles, eyeing Kenan, feeling betrayed. How could he defend that murderer? How could he remain so calm? Maybe it hadn't sunk in yet that Marissa was dead. His roommate could only be in denial for so long with her lifeless body lying on the ground. Logan breathed fast and heavy.

"I swear I didn't kill her, and I know I look guilty as fuck, but I didn't do it! Just think about it. What if you guys came before I did? Then you'd be accused just because someone saw you pulling her out of the water."

Logan looked at Kenan. "Don't fall for that shit. He's playing you."

"Fuck you, dude! I think she drowned. Think about it. If I killed her, why would I stay and drag her ass out the water? My ass would've been gone."

"No where to go, you jackass!" Logan protested.

There should be less talking and more ass whooping.

"If you take a closer look at her, she's been dead for a while. Her body is too cold to just have died now. Maybe he's telling the truth," Kenan said.

Logan shook his head and walked over to the body. *Hell naw*. He ran back to the boys and tackled Adam again. This time Adam fought back. "She has strangled marks around her neck. You're going to fucking hell!"

To Logan's surprise, Kenan punched Adam three times in the face, straight at the nose. He was knocked out with his broken nose crooked and bleeding. Pretty boy wouldn't look attractive any more after they're done with him.

They made their way to Marissa's body; bruises around her neck were imprints of hands. The bruise was black and blue, darker than her blue skin color. Kenan collapsed to his knees. He held her hand, sobbing. Logan ran his fingers over her eyes to close them and removed hair from her face.

May she rest in peace. Logan prayed to himself while he lowered his head to the ground. "I'm sorry, Kenan." He couldn't even imagine how Kenan felt right now. He lost his friend and ex-lover in one fell swoop. Someone died at his vacation home again. Technically, it was the lake this time, but same difference. "Maybe we shouldn't be touching her?"

"What?" Kenan didn't take his eyes off Marissa.

"When the police come, all the evidence will be tampered with. Worst-case scenario, they'll blame us because our fingerprints are all over the body. Will probably take his word over ours in this hick town."

"I'll take my chances. I'm not leaving Mar like this."

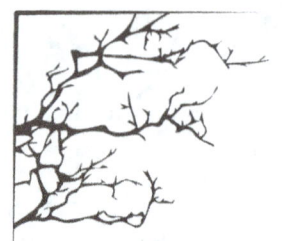

# Chapter Fourteen

All four guys surrounded Marissa's body. Brady had never seen a grown man cry before, but Kenan's eyes were bloodshot red and puffy. The rain poured down heavily resembling standing under a waterfall. Mud soaked between Brady's toes through his flip-flops, and worms invaded the ground.

Marissa's gone. What the hell happened?

She was there last night intimately with Brady. At the time, he could sense someone watching from a distance. Not going to lie, it had aroused him, picturing some female passerby taking a look, possibly masturbating to herself.

So silly now. It made sense that it was Adam; poor Marissa died due to his jealousy. Brady would be next on the list. He gulped. Adam couldn't be trusted. Why did they let a stranger come?

For once in Brady's life, he was speechless. He was the type to say "told you so," but no way would it be appropriate now. He was proud of Kenan knocking the murderer out though. Hopefully, they'd kill Adam before he could end Brady's life.

Tobey broke the ice. "Should we leave her here or carry her to the Jeep? Maybe drive her into town to the hospital or police station?"

Cops always harassed the witnesses, especially the first ones to report a crime because they suspected they actually did it. Brady wasn't going. The police would know they hooked up last night; there's no denying evidence. If Adam didn't get to him first, then Brady would end up in prison.

Brady shook his head and said, "Driving her into town isn't a good idea. We should get her to the cabin though and cover her with a blanket. The rain is washing away all forensics to nail that son of a bitch."

Kenan began to take off his hoodie.

"What are you doing?" Logan asked.

"Covering Marissa's body."

"Are you crazy? You'll be the main target of investigation if she's left with your clothes." Logan frowned. "They'll think you were the last one with Marissa."

"But I wasn't."

Kenan and Tobey shared a look.

Logan glared at his friend. "Do you have proof?"

"I'm not a liar."

"We all know that, but the cops don't. It's better to be safe than sorry."

Kenan put his hoodie back on, this time protecting his head from the downpour. His vacation home didn't have a good track record; no wonder he and Rae abandoned this cursed place.

Rae. Oh no, she couldn't handle losing her best friend, Brady realized. Maybe she could deal if it was an accidental death, but not a brutal murder.

Tobey stood. "There was plastic wrap in that shed we came across. We can cover her with that."

"A shed?" Logan asked.

"Yeah, it's only a little ways from here."

"No. She deserves better than a plastic wrap," Kenan said. "We'll cover her with a blanket."

When A-dumb woke up, Kenan punched him multiple times in the face, knocking him out again. They decided that Kenan and Brady would carry Marissa, it'd be too disrespectful to drag her along the ground, while Logan and Tobey would drag A-dumb, each grabbing one arm. They made sure to make him bump into everything on the ground. No way was he escaping; he'd get the punishment he deserved.

If sensible Kenan hadn't been around, the other guys would've exacted revenge. Eye for an eye; tooth for a tooth.

KENAN TOOK A DEEP BREATH as he placed his hand on the doorknob. He had volunteered to tell the ladies the news and to help them pack, so they could leave right away. Rae needed to hear it from him. No one else.

When he entered the living room, no one was there. The cabin was eerily quiet. Glancing over at the couch gave him chills; Kenan envisioned his mom's tearful gaze before the axe came down on her chest. He shook his head, trying to hide the pain of his past.

He walked up the stairs and found Selma, Naomi, and Rae in Marissa's room. They sat cross-legged on the floor in a circle; they held hands. Naomi was the first to notice Kenan in the doorway. He lowered his eyes to the floor and hung his head down low.

"Where's Marissa? We need to tell her the rules of camping with friends. Possibly put a tracking device on her, so we know where she is at all times because we already know she won't listen to our advice." Naomi smiled.

Kenan didn't believe in stalling or beating around the bush, but he couldn't bring himself to speak up. Why couldn't this morning be a nightmare, and he'd wake up any second? Why did the events have to be real?

"Baby, what's wrong?" Selma asked.

Still no words could escape his mouth. He continued to avoid everyone's gaze.

"Baby, where's Marissa? Where's the guys?"

Kenan gulped. His throat felt like it would tighten and take away his breath. A knot grew in his throat, making it hard to swallow. In any second, he might throw up. He stared at Rae, a tear fell from his eye.

Rae covered her mouth and shook her head, fighting back tears. "She's gone, isn't she?"

Kenan nodded. Rae cried. Her entire body trembled. He ran to his sister and held her in his arms. Naomi and Selma joined in the embrace.

"What happened?" Naomi whispered to him.

"If you're not already packed, you should do it now. We're leaving," Kenan said and stood up.

The three women stared at him in confusion, sadness, and determination in getting the full picture. No one budged. "What happened?" Naomi repeated.

"I'll tell you in the car. Now get moving." They still didn't move, so Kenan added, "Please."

Simultaneously, they rose from the floor. They watched Kenan pull a black blanket off of Marissa's bed.

"I need to see her," Rae said.

"Not like this," Kenan said.

"No, I need to see Marissa." She scurried out the door; Kenan caught her in the hallway. "Let me go! Marissa! Let me go, Kenan!" She struggled to get out of his arms.

He held Rae from the back, loosening his grip when she calmed down. "It's too much if you see her like this. It's too much right now. Trust me." She fell to the floor, causing Kenan to almost trip over her. She sobbed again. He patiently waited for Rae to stop. His heart sank; she was reacting just as he knew she would. Kenan grabbed Naomi's hand. "Please watch Rae while I cover Marissa with this blanket. Then I'll pack your things. Just please stay together and keep Rae in your sights."

Naomi nodded. Kenan didn't think his sister would do anything drastic like commit suicide, but she may be foolish enough to try and run outside again to see Mar's body lying on the porch almost near the back entrance.

He let go of Rae. Naomi bent down to take his place. Selma walked over to Kenan, so he gave her a hug. "It'll be okay." He gave a weak smile, squeezed her hand, then left.

Once outside, Kenan covered Marissa's body. Rain had finally let down a little; too bad it poured non-stop from the time they arrived at the lake to the time they hiked back to the cabin. Couldn't Mother Nature have helped them out?

About a quarter mile into their hike, Adam had woken up. Instead of knocking him out, the boys decided to let him walk on his own while Tobey and Logan guarded him. He had seemed woozy. Who knew, maybe he had a concussion? Kenan didn't mean to get violent like that, but Adam had pushed his buttons. Kenan gave him the benefit of the doubt, then he lied right to his face. Not cool to piss off the guy who may be on his side, therefore, keeping the mob away. Tobey, Logan, and Brady had wanted to kill him, and Kenan was sure the women would agree.

Guys were easier to express reason with than girls. Exhibit A: the guys followed Kenan's orders with no hesitation even though distraught. Exhibit B: when the girls heard the news, they acted like zombies in a daze, rebelling against his orders, being defiant until they got the answers they wanted.

Selma, Naomi, and Rae better straighten up in case something else endangering might happen, or they'd get themselves, or someone else, killed.

The four boys stood around in a circle on the porch, blocking Adam's escape route.

"How did they take it?" Tobey asked.

"Just make sure they don't see Mar's body. I have to go back inside to pack their bags." Kenan walked back inside and found Selma in the living room. "I thought I told you to stay with Rae."

"No, you told Naomi that. What happened to Marissa?"

"We don't have time for that. We need to pack then leave."

Selma grabbed his face with both of her soft hands. "You don't need to protect me; I won't break. What happened to Marissa?"

Kenan took a deep breath. "We found Adam pulling her out of the lake. At first, we thought she drowned, but..." He sniffed.

"But what?" Selma asked softly.

"She had hand marks around her neck, like someone strangled her."

Selma covered her mouth, wide-eyed. She gasped. "You guys think Adam did it?"

"...He was there."

She nodded and looked angry. Kenan was aware of her I-want-to-kick-someone's-butt expression. "Why did she have to pick that loser up at the parking lot?"

Kenan frowned. "Don't blame the victim."

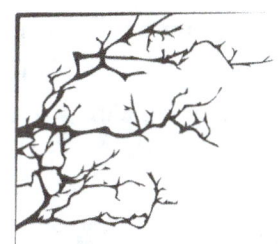

# Chapter Fifteen

Naomi grew impatient inside the Jeep. Someone's death was an emergency. Why was everyone diddle-daddling? She refused to look out the window, refused to peek over at Marissa's body under the blanket. It taunted her like one of Edgar Allan Poe's creations. It didn't feel right leaving Marissa alone like this. What if a bear or wolf mauled her or something?

What if this was all a sick prank? Marissa was under the blanket laughing her butt off, then she'd pop up and scream "boo," scaring the girls on purpose. That would explain why no one hauled ass.

Naomi rubbed Rae's arm. She nestled her head on Naomi's chest. Her best friend had completely shut down. She didn't talk to anyone, didn't make eye contact with Tobey or Brady, the people in the front seats of the vehicle.

"Let's go, baby," Naomi ordered from the back seat.

Tobey looked at her through the rearview mirror. "Jeep won't start."

"Excuse me?" Brady asked.

"Jeep won't start." Tobey exited the vehicle from the driver's side and joined Kenan outside. They both looked under the hood.

"What the hell is going on?" Naomi asked, talking to herself. She wiped a tear that strolled down her cheek.

Brady leaned in the passenger seat. He sighed and turned his body to face the girls. He rubbed Rae's knee. "It'll be okay. I promise we'll get out of here."

No reaction from her whatsoever. No blink of an eye. No sniff. No nod or shake of the head. Absolutely nothing.

It seemed like Tobey and Kenan were outside for an eternity. "Brady, go out there to see what they're saying."

He saluted. When his fingers left his forehead, droplets of water sprinkled on Naomi and Rae's clothes. "Yes ma'am." He got out of the Jeep.

Naomi sighed, rubbing the tiny stains from her shirt. It seemed like another eternity, then Logan, Adam, and Selma left the other Jeep to stand outside as well. Logan had yanked Adam from his seat and was pulling him by the arm. Unfortunately, when they joined the others in front of the popped hood, Naomi couldn't read any facial expressions, but she could see someone pacing back and forth, while others had wild hand gestures.

This couldn't be good.

Rae closed her eyes. "We're not getting out of here, are we?"

"Yes, we are," Naomi said.

Rae snickered. If she didn't stop talking like that, people would think she snapped. In fact, she scared Naomi—the way she was out of it. Being here was too much for her, and it was all Naomi's fault.

Naomi opened the door to get fresh air and to eavesdrop. But, everyone stopped chatting and went off in different directions. Tobey and Logan carried Adam into the house.

Kenan walked to the Jeep's door and leaned into it. "Rae, are you okay?"

She turned to face him. "We're not getting out of here, are we?"

He closed his eyes and took a deep breath. "Someone took the belts out of the Jeeps."

"Excuse me?" Naomi's eyes widened.

"Someone—"

"It's time to tell us what happened to Marissa right now. We have a right to know. Are we in danger?"

Naomi wished that her boyfriend were here with her. Why did he act like Adam's bodyguard? A light bulb went off in her head, but she couldn't quite put all the pieces together. Did Adam have something to do with Marissa's death?

"She drowned, or someone threw her in the water after strangling her," Kenan said.

"She was murdered?" Rae covered her mouth, tears slid down her cheeks. "Kenan, it's happening again."

He bent down and held his sister's hand. "No Rae. We caught Adam red-handed. He can't hurt anyone else."

"You saw him kill Marissa?" Naomi asked.

"Not exactly." Kenan scratched his head. "We saw him pulling her out of the lake."

Naomi sighed. "He warned us at the store. Why didn't we take him serious-ly?"

"What do you mean?" Kenan asked.

"We were in the parking lot, and he picked on Marissa for trusting him. Said he was crazy with that stupid smirk on his face. Personally, I thought he was lame, but now I see he was hinting the truth, and I feel so bad that I didn't listen."

Kenan rubbed his eyes. "I wish someone would've told me or one of the other guys."

"It's not like you would've left him in the parking lot, forcing him to hitch-hike home."

"No, but I certainly wouldn't have allowed him to be alone with Mar. Maybe all this would've been avoided."

How dare he imply it was Naomi's fault? What if everyone did?

If Adam killed Marissa, then he probably messed with the transportation to ensure no one could leave. He wasn't finished having fun yet. He would try to execute them one by one; Naomi was too young to die. She deserved to have a peaceful death, falling asleep and never waking up at the age of ninety-nine or one-hundred.

In a panic, she pulled her cell phone out of her purse. She dialed 911. No signal bars. It took all of Naomi not to toss it out the window. "This can't be happening!" She began to cry. Rae enveloped her arms around Naomi.

"All we can do is wait for RL. He should be here soon," Kenan said.

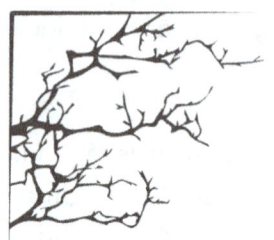

# Chapter Sixteen

Adam flinched in pain when he touched his broken nose. His handsome face was ruined. He'd forever be damaged, no amount of plastic surgery could fix his nose. No amount of therapy could restore his dignity. They thought he was capable of murder. How dare they!

Adam grew up around civilization and had a decent childhood. He was exposed to worldly things and knew how to act like a gentleman. Not these West Virginia hillbillies. If anyone were capable of murder, it'd be one of them. They grew up in the country with nothing to do but torment animals and insects for fun. Plus, they knew how to navigate around the woods. Adam had no idea, but these hicks couldn't understand logic.

It was hard for him to breathe; if he got out of this alive, the first thing he'd do would be visit the hospital, then go to the police. All Adam wanted to do this weekend was have fun, party, get drunk, possibly a little high, and get laid. Now the fate of his life was in the hands of people who probably couldn't count past twenty.

Tobey, the quiet one, stared at him as though he was a piece of meat.

*Please make it out alive. Please make it out alive. Please make it out alive.* His heartbeat quickened. What if they believed in getting their own justice without going to the cops first? If so, he was screwed. He surveyed the room, trying to find any potential weapons, but the room was empty except for the old furniture. Not even any paintings hung on the walls.

Even though Kenan attacked Adam, he could probably reason with him. Maybe there was hope. Adam doubted he could convince him that he was innocent because it was much easier to blame 'the stranger,' yet he could point out that they'd all go to prison for murder instead of him. Then maybe they'd reconsider their plan.

Adam assumed he was dragged inside to be taken care of.

He gulped. He was too young to die over something so wrong. He knew he couldn't voice it, or else Logan would pounce on him before he could get the first syllable out of his mouth. Adam glanced over at Tobey. If only they'd speak, so Adam could know where their heads were. Talk about a terrible hangover!

Why hadn't he texted, emailed, or called his friends to let them know he left the state with strangers? At least, his friends would've known where to find him. Now, the local authorities would just call his body 'John Doe' after stealing his money and expensive assets.

Why did Marissa, the reason Adam came on the trip in the first place, have to die? No wonder he looked guilty. Someone would need to talk soon, or he'd die from a panic attack. No one tied him up, but Adam wouldn't dare run because he knew these guys could catch him.

Where could he escape to anyway? Unlikely he knew how to get to the main road or the neighbor's backyard. Heck, in these parts, homeowners probably shot whoever passed their 'No Trespassing' signs on their property.

"Why did you kill Marissa?" Logan asked.

The calm before the storm, Adam assumed.

"I didn't."

"Where did you put both belts?"

"What?"

"Where's the fucking Jeep belts that you stole from under the hood? What did you do with them?"

"I don't even know what you're talking about," Adam said.

"There's no point talking to him. He'll deny everything. Won't help him live though." Tobey cracked his knuckles. No emotion whatsoever. How could they be cool about killing a human being? They were animals, cruel animals.

No way could Adam get out of this predicament now. They accused him of stealing car parts? Did it really look like he was a mechanic? Great, so if he did happen to escape, there'd be no point because he couldn't drive away. Who would mess with the transportation? Probably the same person who killed Marissa, and as long as they blamed Adam, they all were in danger.

They blamed the wrong guy.

Sweat dripped down Adam's forehead; his body trembled against his wet clothes that felt like wet cement weighing him down. "You gonna kill me, Tobey? Are you gonna be the brave soul who ends my life? Well guess what, you'll get life. I'll haunt you forever."

"I hope Marissa haunts your ass," Tobey said.

"Won't be time for that," Logan added.

Adam closed his eyes, a tear rolled down his cheek. "I hope she haunts me too, so she can tell me who really killed her."

"That's rich. You're really gonna deny it, you scumbag. They caught you red-handed!"

"No, you saw me pulling her out of the water. I got there literally minutes before you did. If Kenan or you would've found her first, then you guys would've been in my predicament."

Tobey blinked. "Marissa."

"What?" Adam asked.

"Marissa. Use her fucking name. You keep using 'she' and 'her' to put distance between you, like killers do with their victims. Use her name. She was our friend and deserves respect," Tobey said.

Adam couldn't stop sweating, which made his body odor even worse. He needed a shower. Why did he get wasted last night to the point he stayed in that raggedy, old shed? He shouldn't have let that skank upset him that much. He wasn't used to this. Adam was used to being primped and taking hours to perfect his metrosexual look in the mirror before leaving his apartment.

Now, Adam's hair was wet and stringy, his breath and armpits stunk, his clothes were caked with mud, and he didn't even want to think of the possible bugs crawling on him. He was embarrassed that he'd get bumped off this way.

"I just met Marissa. Why would I kill her?"

Logan raised an eyebrow. "Why would *we*?"

That was a good question. Adam knew he didn't do it, but he had no idea why her friends would. They all seemed to get along, too well in Brady's case. He was desperate to get the hillbillies off his back. He'd do anything, even throw someone under the bus. "Maybe Brady did it. He hooked up with Marissa last night; maybe she threatened to tell, and he got carried away. Or maybe they've had a love affair for a while, and she confessed to being pregnant. He flips out, not wanting to be a dad, then bang she's dead." Adam frowned. "I mean, Marissa's dead."

He knew it was a long shot, but that's all he had at the moment.

"How do you know they hooked up?" Logan asked, out of curiosity. If it was under better circumstances, then they all could participate in boy's locker room gossip. Unfortunately, it would never be like that now.

"I saw them. That's when I went to the shed to drink my sorrows away. I didn't mean to fall asleep there, but I did."

Logan and Tobey made eye contact. Maybe he was getting through to them. Maybe he wouldn't need Kenan after all. They walked away to huddle but stayed close enough to Adam. They tried to whisper, yet he could still hear them. The consequence of a deathly silent cabin with too much open area.

"What do you think?" Logan asked.

"Brady and I did come across a shed with a Moonshine jar open. It was close enough to the lake that his story could be true."

"Then he blacked-out and doesn't remember."

Oh, shit. Were they kidding Adam? No matter what, they'd blame him. Adam hadn't blacked-out since his damn fraternity days. He knew how to be more responsible now.

"What about Brady?" Tobey asked.

Logan gave Adam a mean stare as if challenging him, then faced Tobey again. "I don't know. We should ask Brady if last night is true, but I still don't think he killed her. Jackass over there is just grasping for straws. He's getting desperate." Logan smirked. "By the end of our conversation, he'll have a magical theory of why each of us did it too."

Tobey nodded.

Kenan entered the living room. He rubbed his forehead and squatted down, so he was eye level to Adam. "Yesterday did you tell the girls that Marissa should've done a background check on you because you're dangerous?"

Of course, that idiotic prank would bite him in the ass, he scolded himself. "It was a joke. Ask any of them; they didn't take it seriously because it wasn't meant to be."

"Well, if they did, then Marissa may still be alive," Kenan said.

"I didn't kill her. Kenan, listen to me, man; it wasn't me. If anyone is capable of murder, it'd be Brady."

Tobey tapped Kenan on the shoulder. They huddled by the front door. Logan stood as watchdog, eyeing Adam like he was a mastermind killer.

Instead of coming over, Tobey and Kenan went outside. What were they up to? Soon, Naomi and Brady followed them back into the living room. Was everyone going to get their turn? For Adam's last minutes on earth, could he see the beautiful Selma?

Brady, with fiery eyes, sprinted towards Adam and knelt down in his face. His cheeks were flushed angry red. "You motherfucker, I didn't kill Marissa."

"You fucked her then killed her," Adam said.

"Did you two hook up last night at the lake?" Logan asked.

Brady punched his own hand. "No."

Adam shook his head. "You fucking liar!"

"Why would I have sex with Marissa?"

"Naomi told us that you told everyone you had a crush on Marissa during our ride here. Maybe you finally decided to make your move," Logan said.

"That's a lie. I never said that. Kenan back me up," Brady pleaded.

"He never said that."

"And Marissa and I talked until Kenan met up with us. When I left, she was alive. Right?"

"Yeah she was. In fact, Adam was the last one with her, and if he's convinced they hooked up, that's motive. He would've been jealous, drunk, and acted on his anger," Kenan said.

Since when was Adam the last guy to see Marissa? He remembered being angry. He wanted to confront her, but liquor took care of that. He was too wasted to move. Or was he? Oh no, what if he did black-out?

Forget that, Adam decided. He didn't kill Marissa. These assholes were pathological liars, untruths rolled right off their tongues as though lying was their first language. And they got a pass because they were buddies. No one blinked an eye that Naomi started shit. No one cared that Brady lied. The stupid prick. Since Brady didn't tell the truth, he had something to hide.

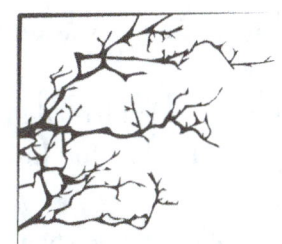

# Chapter Seventeen

"Why would you do that? Why would you lie on me?" Brady asked, defeated. He looked at Naomi, who held Tobey's hand. She buried her face in his white/black striped shirt. His question was met with muteness, which pissed him off. "Huh? Why did you lie?"

"She didn't mean any harm." Tobey came to the rescue. Any other time, Naomi would have a lot to say; now all of a sudden, cat had her tongue. She didn't mean any harm. Whatever.

She could have gotten Brady killed. What if the guys believed Adam because of her damn fabrication? Then he'd be tied up alongside A-dumb. It wasn't safe to explode on her, not with her boyfriend there. So not fair.

He staggered upstairs, holding onto the rail. Luckily, he made it into the bathroom. He shut and locked the door. Brady vomited in the toilet, his body convulsed.

Afterwards, he made his way to the sink and knelt down, letting water splash on his face. He looked in the mirror and panted. It was hard to breathe properly. Fun and games were over the second they found Marissa dead. He didn't enjoy how serious the weekend turned. It didn't sit right with him.

He had to fib about having sex with Marissa to protect himself. It wasn't even about staying in good graces with Rae. Brady could sense everyone turning on each other down the line when paranoia sank in, especially if A-dumb could get inside their heads. Did he have anything to lose?

Brady was the reason Marissa had died. That psycho had killed her out of a jealous rage. His heart sank. Poor Marissa. She had thought he liked her as more than a friend. Her seducing him all made sense. Her teasing about him being jealous in the store all made sense.

Brady covered his mouth, then spun around, aiming for the toilet. He threw up once more. That psycho wasn't finished because he stole the belts. He planned to toy with them until he was ready to strike again, and there was no place to hide.

What if they had the wrong guy? Brady doubted A-dumb could pull off destroying the Jeeps alone. Then again, maybe he wasn't stupid. He had hid his past for a reason.

Brady was terrified of dying. Someone in the cabin was a killer, and he knew it wasn't him. There were people downstairs who disliked him; would they even have his back in a crisis? Was he next on the killer's list? He remembered Kenan's joke about how his movie wouldn't kill the black people first. Brady threw up again, then sat on the tiled floor. He rocked back and forth.

He wished he was exaggerating, but his gut instinct told him to watch his back. No one was in the clear. He could understand Adam grasping for straws, trying to take the blame off himself. What if he didn't do it? What if he honestly thought Brady had killed Marissa?

Brady had left Marissa with Kenan. What if they hooked up, and she threatened to ruin his relationship with Selma? What if he strangled her to death to keep his secret?

He shook his head. Kenan had said he left her with Adam. Unless Kenan was lying. For survival reasons, it had been easy for him to lie. Maybe Kenan did the same to protect himself.

Brady didn't feel comfortable ending Adam's life anymore, or being a witness. He could go to prison for that too. Heck, he needed to make it out alive first.

Brady scanned the bathroom for any potential weapons, but didn't see anything in plain view. He crawled to the bottom cabinet and found nothing, not even a toenail clipper or nail filer.

How long could he hide? Would anyone check up on him? Or would he be forgotten like Marissa and Adam were? How did a group of people not realize two people were missing? Then again, Rae had managed to escape the cabin too. If Brady was crazy, he could've killed her and disposed the body. No one would have been any the wiser.

Maybe that's how the killer got around. Chills ran down Brady's spine. Did the murderer watch him and Rae sleep in the Jeep? Did he pass the vehicle to walk inside the cabin, and if one of them happened to look up at the right moment, they would have caught him without realizing it?

What if a guy didn't kill Marissa? What if a girl did? Women were irrational nowadays; crazies had pretty good strength to fight whomever. *Snapped* was a popular show for a reason. Could a female really remove the belts though? Maybe his friend's killer and the thief weren't the same person?

If the group were dealing with two different crazies, then that was even worse. Never in a million years would Brady think he'd be afraid to be around a group of people that he knew for a while.

Brady's heartbeat quickened when he thought he heard the floorboard creak outside the bathroom door. Wide-eyed, he held his breath. What if the killer, or killers, were outside the door, plotting to get in, so he would be the second victim? When he didn't hear anything else, he cursed himself for letting his mind run with fear. He needed to man up and look after Rae. He didn't know what he'd do if anything bad were to happen to her.

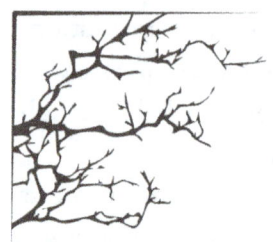

# Chapter Eighteen

Rae sat in the Jeep's back seat while Selma stood by the open door. Selma was the last person she wanted to be near. "I don't need a baby-sitter." In no way, shape, or form did Selma care about Rae; besides she had hated Marissa, so Rae knew she didn't give a lick that she was gone forever.

Marissa. She was there yesterday. Her best friend. Dead. Worm food. Rae wanted to cry herself to sleep, but she wouldn't give Selma the satisfaction of watching her suffer. Rae swore if she saw her smirk, then she'd kick her butt.

Selma rolled her eyes. "Tell your brother that. He's the one who asked me to look over you." Really? This bitch had the nerve to be rude to someone grieving, Rae thought.

"Great to know it's not on your priority list."

"You know what, it isn't. Buck up. People have better things to do than watch you mope around. I could be searching for those belts, trying to get answers from Adam. Anything productive. Not this."

"Get the fuck away from me."

"Why do you hate me? I've never done anything to you."

"Really? You want to share an afterschool special moment with me now." Rae slapped her forehead in frustration. "Newsflash! My fucking best friend just died! She was fucking killed, and we're all gonna die! So fuck you and your questions. I'm taking my answers to the grave."

Selma struck her. It felt like ten-thousand yellow jackets stung her all at once. Caught off guard, Rae held her cheek. She punched Selma in the stomach.

"You bitch!" Selma wrestled her inside the Jeep. They scratched each other and pulled each other's hair. They were relentless in their attack. Rae didn't care about the pain; she was getting her aggression and frustration out.

Rae imagined her brother's girlfriend as the stealthy killer. As far as she knew, Kenan had spent alone time with Marissa. Selma would have been jealous. What if she confronted Marissa? Knowing her friend, she would have been a smart ass, causing Selma to snap and kill her. Kenan loved Selma. What if he was covering for her?

Rae hadn't seen Marissa's body, but she heard all the murmurs surrounding her. They had said she was strangled to death. At this exact moment, Selma had her hands around Rae's neck. A coincidence? She didn't think so.

Any other time, Rae would have given up and welcomed her death, but not now. She had to see Selma suffer, had to put her through hell. Rae let out a loud scream, which gave her the strength to kick her opponent in the stomach. Selma flew backwards, landing on the ground. Rae jumped on top of her.

They rolled around in the mud; their clothes got filthy dirty. Rae snatched her hand out of Selma's grip and blocked her eyes from the sun. No, it wasn't the sun because the silver with blue specs twinkle was too low to the ground, she reasoned. Selma kept fighting when Rae had clearly stopped, so Rae yelled, "Stop bitch!" She whacked Selma hard, then stood to run to the light. Selma followed her.

Behind high grass shrubs, the belts were sliced into small cubes. The evidence, a.k.a. knife, was placed right beside the mess. Rae wiped tears from her eyes, dropping to the ground. Their way to escape was destroyed. Selma fell down beside her and gasped. They held each other.

Rae's aggressive energy vanished.

"No, no, no. Our only way to escape." Selma screeched.

It was official; she, her friends, and Selma were going to be tormented at this very cabin. And there was nothing she could do about it. Or was there? "I know my way around the area. I can walk or run outta here."

"There's no way this is happening."

"It is if someone drove away for privacy. Or found a hiding place. If someone drove away though, then that means..."

Selma looked at Rae, waiting for an answer, impatiently. "What?"

"Unless...someone outside our group is messing with us. If they're locals, they know their way around these woods too; it wouldn't be hard for them to park off the grid, mess with our Jeeps, ride off, and then come back. Real easy. Or it could be the guy who led us here. It's been way past morning, and he still hasn't arrived yet." Rae scanned the area, holding herself. "What if he did come a long time ago, but parked far away to go unnoticed? What if he's been watching us all this time? He never wanted to buy our land; he just wanted to torture us."

Selma eyed her suspiciously. "So you don't think Adam did it?"

"I'm just looking at all angles."

Selma folded her arms across her chest. "I think you did it."

"What?"

"I think you did it. You're putting on an act about being sad. You killed Marissa. You practically admitted to Naomi and me this morning. You didn't see signs or have visions." She pointed an accusatory finger at Rae. "You hinted what you did to your *so-called friend*."

Rae stood. "If you suspect someone, it's best not to say it to their face. You'll be added to their list quicker."

"Or they'll know someone's on to them, so they'll behave until they feel safe to strike again. By then, I'll be outta here. Don't think I won't defend myself."

"You killed Mar! You choked her to death, just like you choked me."

"That's ridiculous!"

Letting her anger subside, it dawned on Rae that Selma believed it could have been someone other than Adam. Did the group think that too?

Rae turned, walking away. "For future reference, don't think I'll have trouble defending myself."

"I'm keeping my eye on you!" Leaves crushed under both their feet while Selma ran after her. She grabbed Rae by the arm. "Wait!"

Rae yanked her arm away. "Don't touch me."

"I'm not a killer."

"Well, neither am I."

Both women put their hands on their hips and stared each other down. If it was a Western, they'd have their guns drawn and whoever survived won. "I know a way we can catch the person," Selma said.

"How?"

There wasn't really a way to trap yourself. Of course, if Selma were the killer, she'd want to devise a plan where no one looked at her as a suspect. Rae had just admitted to finding her guilty, so she wanted to shift the blame to someone else. Then again, maybe Selma was sincere. If she wanted to kill Rae, now would be the time, while they were alone. She could easily lie and say Rae had snapped, so she murdered her in self-defense, if Selma were clever. Rae leaned toward no, she wasn't that bright.

"Only the car thief and killer, if they're the same person, would know the hiding place of the parts or what was used to slice everything. We don't tell anyone, then if we hear someone mention it, we know they're guilty."

"Not even Kenan?" Rae asked.

"Not even Kenan." Selma held out her finger, so they could pinky swear. Rae knew she could keep this to herself. She couldn't trust that Selma would. For all Rae knew, she could tell someone trying to set them up by having them say it aloud to Rae—not knowing any better—then Rae would get off her scent. Or someone could stumble upon it accidentally as they had. Then they'd be blamed even though they were innocent.

"Should we move it?" Rae asked.

"I'm not touching it and putting my fingerprints all over evidence, but we should buck up because that was our only way out. Do you really think you can get out of here? Call for help or something?"

"I don't see why I couldn't."

"I would go, but I'd just slow you down, and I want to get out of here as soon as possible."

Rae nodded. "I should go."

"Wait. You can't. Kenan would never forgive me if I let you out of my sight."

Rae smirked. "But he'd forgive you for fighting his sister?"

Selma looked concerned and frightened. "Are you gonna tell him?"

"No because then I'd have to explain why we stopped, which would lead to a conversation about these bushes. Besides, I really don't want to hear a ten-hour lecture on the art of friendship. Do you?"

Selma giggled, shaking her head.

"We need to stop them from torturing Adam. If they kill him, then they aren't any better than those animals ten years ago," Rae whispered.

They treaded up towards the cabin. Selma headed for the front entrance, yet Rae proceeded the back way. "Where are you going?" Selma asked.

Rae paused, turning around. "I don't go that way."

"Why?"

"You wouldn't understand." Rae lowered her eyes to the ground. She picked at dry mud on her shirt and yoga pants. "We should really take a shower."

"That's rich, trying to change the subject. You don't know if I'd understand or not because you won't let me in."

Why should Rae? Selma had just confessed that she thought Rae had killed her own best friend. So yeah, she wouldn't let Selma in. She was up to something; Rae wasn't fooled. For someone wanting to leave this place, Selma surely talked her out of running right this second. Someone in a panic would've encouraged Rae to go. Heck, they would've tagged along.

But not Selma. Probably because she's the murderer or knows who is, so she feels comfortable, knowing nothing will happen to her. Then again, Selma's not an actress; she really sold being devastated when they had found that knife and pile of parts.

The knife. "We should go back and get the knife as a weapon," Rae said.

Both ladies turned their head to look at the bushes. "Where would we hide it? It's not like it'll fit in our pants."

"Just forget I mentioned it then." Rae folded her arms across her chest and rolled her eyes. Someone worried for her safety didn't seem to want to protect herself with a weapon. So fishy.

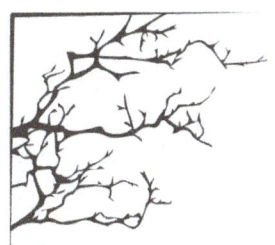

# Chapter Nineteen

Naomi felt icky in this tacky, abandoned building. She could feel the creepy crawlers and Hepatitis C entering her body. She hated it and was confused how her boyfriend could be relaxed inside. Tobey steadily looked for rope while she stood by the front door. "Earlier today, Brady wouldn't leave the doorway either," he said.

Typical Brady being lazy and making someone else do all the hard work. Naomi held herself. She couldn't believe that their friend was dead. Adam was adamant he didn't do it. What if he was telling the truth? Then that meant another good friend was a killer. She shivered, trying to get that image out of her head.

Someone destroyed their getaway. Naomi had a sickening feeling that it wasn't some cruel, out of hand, practical joke. The killer wasn't finished, and he was toying with them. Breaking them down with psychological warfare. Well, it was working on her; she was afraid to die.

The killer was so quiet that he could easily sneak up on people. He was able to kill Marissa without any witnesses; plus, he was able to destroy the Jeeps without anyone noticing. The Quiet Killer or The Silencer. If they all passed away, Naomi could see Hollywood playing it as a horror movie trilogy. Unfortunately, she wouldn't be around to see if that would be the case.

How could Rae or Brady not hear anything? How could they not feel the Jeeps moving? Unless the killer had operated when no one was around. But how? When? If Naomi wouldn't get answers soon, she'd go crazy. "If Adam didn't kill Marissa, then who did?" she asked.

Tobey stopped searching through the red toolbox. He walked in her direction and stood in front of her. He stepped closer in a forward motion, causing Naomi to take a step back. She almost bumped into the wall. Thankfully, she didn't. Who knew what kind of bacteria was on those walls. She couldn't afford to get a skin disease or stain her designer clothes.

"Of course Adam did it," Tobey said.

"What if he didn't?"

"He did."

Naomi sighed. "What if he didn't...maybe Brady did it, like Adam said." She knew she was grasping at straws, but maybe Adam was right. Brady was sketchy. He could've hid the belts before Rae snuck out of the cabin to sleep with him. And just because Tobey had escorted him back, didn't mean that Brady couldn't have gone back to the lake after Kenan and Adam left.

Maybe he finally snapped because he was tired of people picking on him. Naomi was the biggest offender of that. She'd have to watch her back around Brady.

"We can't turn on each other; that's what Adam wants," Tobey said calmly. She noticed that her boyfriend didn't protest that Brady didn't do it. Goodness gracious, what if she was next on his hit list?

It was hard for her to catch her breath. She grabbed her throat as if choking to death.

He ran his fingers through her hair. The gesture soothed her, so she breathed more slowly.

"I can't lose you, Naomi. You're my everything."

"How are we going to get out of here?"

"We'll find those missing parts and put the Jeeps back together, or we may have to walk outta here. Either way, we're escaping. I'm not letting anything bad happen to you." Tobey wrapped his arms around Naomi. She rested her head on his chest. She couldn't imagine life without him, and he couldn't imagine life without her. If they got out of this alive, then she planned to propose to Tobey. Life was too short to pass opportunities up.

She never would've imagined that they'd be spending their two-year anniversary in fear.

He was right. If they were going to make it out alive, then they had to stick together. If they had each other's back, then the killer couldn't strike again. Not with everyone on high alert. If only they would have stayed as a group at the lake, then Marissa wouldn't be gone right now. Everything was so surreal.

Naomi never wanted Tobey to let her go; she could surrender in his arms forever. Now wasn't the time to get intimate, but Naomi couldn't help herself.

The fear built up inside was becoming overbearing and making her aroused. It also didn't help that her boyfriend wore her favorite cologne.

She raised her head to nuzzle his neck, giving Tobey sweet kisses.

"There's never a dull moment with you. First, you can't breathe, now you're horny."

"How do you know I'm horny?" Naomi licked his neck.

"I know you better than you know yourself." He backed away, holding both of Naomi's hands. They locked gazes. "I want nothing more than to be with you, but not here." He looked around the ugly space. "Not like this."

Naomi sniffed. "I wanna go home."

Tobey went back to holding Naomi, her tears soaked his shirt. "We will be soon. I promise you, Omi."

She knew he was trying to help. It did work a little. As long as he was by her side, she'd be okay. Tobey was her protector, her rock, which she wouldn't trade for anything else in the world.

Tobey instructed Naomi to stay close to the group and never wander alone. If she had to use the bathroom, take a shower, any solitary event, then take at least one person with her. Someone she trusted. Someone who would have her back. She kept nodding, letting the information soak in. She tried to remain strong, so he'd feel comfortable enough to leave her side and continue looking for rope. They needed to tie Adam up until they could figure out a permanent solution.

Adam was off the list of people she trusted for obvious reasons. She didn't trust Selma as far as she could throw her, which wouldn't be far. Naomi was petite while Selma was curvy like J Lo or Kim Kardashian, ladies who didn't think they were fat. Newsflash: they were. She didn't trust Brady either because he'd only look out for himself.

That only left Tobey, Logan, Rae, and Kenan. Good thing she never pissed off the strong men, so they wouldn't hesitate to have her back.

"Are you scared?" Naomi asked. Someone didn't want anyone to escape their location. That was a big deal.

"We caught Adam. I'm not scared. I'm pissed off." Tobey didn't have any luck finding rope in the toolbox, so he moved on to the cabinets. He stopped at one in particular and pulled an object out. "Lookey here what I found." He turned around, holding the flashlight in plain view.

"What is it doing here?"

"Adam must have hid it. It was behind some bottles and jars like he didn't want anyone to find it."

Naomi wiped tears from her eyes. "I feel so bad for not believing him when he said he was crazy. If I would've told someone, Marissa would still be alive."

"Don't do that. It's not your fault. You thought he was joking. Crazy people barely mention that, so how were you supposed to know he was serious?"

Good ole Tobey, always trying to make Naomi feel better, but not this time. She couldn't erase the guilt and regret from her heart, no matter how hard she tried.

Tobey crossed the room and sighed. He lifted Naomi's chin with his finger. They gazed into each other's eyes. "I'm sorry about Marissa; I know you two were good friends."

Naomi felt a knot in her throat. She never got to tell Marissa how much she enjoyed her company because she was busy frontin'. Now, Marissa would never know. All because she was jealous of Marissa and Rae's bond. So many things left unsaid. "I'm sorry you lost her as a friend too."

"I know Rae and Kenan are taking it pretty hard. Kenan can barely keep himself together, probably blames himself for leaving Adam alone with her, but he didn't know Adam was crazy either."

"Yeah, he shouldn't blame himself."

"You shouldn't either," he said firmly, trying to get through her thick skull. Her boyfriend knew her all too well.

Naomi gulped. "What happens if we can't find rope?"

"I don't know. We'd have to figure out something. Kenan seems to think killing him is out of the question."

"You guys weren't really planning to kill him, were you?"

Tobey's silence was all the answer that Naomi needed. She shivered. She wasn't a cold-blooded killer, revenge or no revenge. She hadn't known the man she loved and slept beside every night was capable of it.

Was Tobey changing right before her eyes, or was he always like that?

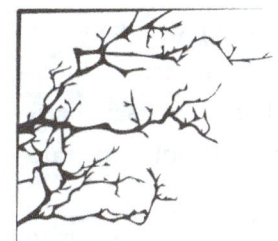

# Chapter Twenty

Selma was taking a much needed hot shower, probably the same as Rae. Kenan stood over the see-through shower curtain. "Does Rae seem okay to you?" he asked.

How convenient that Rae had already thought of her cover story. She wasn't fooling anyone asking about the man who was supposed to sign the deed. If only Selma could express her concerns to Kenan, but he wouldn't even entertain the thought. If anyone ever badmouthed Rae, he always acted as if it was a huge betrayal.

"If anything, she may be experiencing PTSD," Selma answered.

"Like what soldiers go through?"

"Yeah, it can happen to anyone who experienced something devastating in their life."

"I should talk to her."

*Try not to get yourself killed.*

"Go ahead." She was tired of hearing about Rae this and Rae that. She wished Kenan would focus more on her. He never once asked how she felt about today. How she was holding up. Was he still mad at her for cocking an attitude about him coming in late last night? Could he really blame her? Kenan had been out all night with his ex. Hello, Selma was tough but it would still feel nice to know that her baby cared about her feelings.

"I'll go after you get out." Kenan hadn't noticed the hint of frustration in Selma's voice, unless he chose the easy approach of ignoring it. Typical male behavior.

"I can take care of myself."

"What's your problem?"

"Oh I don't know. I'm stuck in this hell hole with crazy people, not only insane but murderers."

"We caught Adam."

"Do you really think he killed Marissa?" No one could be trusted at this point, she thought. She would have to keep an eye out for everyone, including Kenan. If he wasn't on the same page, then she needed to distance herself, better protection that way. He could walk them right into a trap without him realizing it.

Rae thought Selma was the killer. Did she already express that to Kenan? Did he stand up for Selma, if so?

"If not Adam, then who? I'm assuming you already have theories since you asked," Kenan said.

The water falling on her felt like a warm, tickling massage. That would be the only thing pleasant coming from this room after her comment. "Rae *claims*—"

"Claims!"

"Let me finish." Selma rolled her eyes. "Your sister *claims* that she left here to sleep with Brady. Well, no one knows technically when she left. She could have had time to see Marissa at the lake before going to him. He said he'd been laying down, so Brady wouldn't have noticed."

Kenan whipped the shower curtain back, darting for her naked body. With threatening eyes, he grabbed Selma by the arms and pinned her up against the slippery wall. "How dare you blame Rae? She didn't do it."

"You don't know that." Selma refused to back down even though she never seen this violent, aggressive side of her boyfriend. If she had to, she'd fight back physically.

"I swear to God, Selma, if you turn the group against Rae, I will—"

"Will what? Kill me?" Her body tensed. "Huh? Will you kill me?"

Kenan cracked his neck. "Rae's not a killer. She's been through a lot and doesn't need your bullshit."

"Are you a killer?" She noticed he didn't object to that statement.

He squeezed tighter on Selma's arms. "How can you ask me that? You're demented."

"Let go of me."

"Or what?" Kenan smirked. "Will you kill me?"

Selma winced with disgust. "It's funny that you ask me that because *your* sister thinks I killed Marissa." His grip didn't loosen; Kenan didn't change facial expressions or anything. Of course, Saint Rae could accuse whomever she want-

ed. This pissed Selma off. "Why don't you go roughen her up? Call her demented for giving an opinion? She took it way better than you when I accused her
by the way."

"You told her? She doesn't need extra stress, you bitch!"

Bitch. Kenan had to know that would push Selma's buttons. She tried to
slap his face, but he wouldn't let go. She couldn't wiggle out of his grip, which
angered her even more, so she did the next best thing. Selma spat in his direction. Her saliva landed on his face above his upper lip.

In shock, Kenan stood frozen. He wiped his face; she took the opportunity
with her free arm to lift it up and smack him in the face. She closed her eyes,
waiting for his fist.

Kenan punched the wall right near the side of Selma's head. He grabbed her
again and lifted her off the tub floor. "You disgusting pig. Oink. Oink."

"Let go of me!" She turned her head to avoid his gaze.

"Mess with Rae again and then you'll have to answer to me." Kenan
dropped her.

Selma slipped and fell hard on her butt with her legs open in the air. She
also hit her head against the surface. "Ouch."

Kenan laughed and stomped, almost crushing her vagina. "Be careful, you
don't want to get a concussion. Who knows, since I'm a *killer*, I probably
planned it. Not all murders have to be bloody and gruesome."

Selma held the back of her head and sobbed. "We're done!" She spat again,
but it missed him.

He chuckled. "Oink, oink, oink." He gave her the evil eye, then left out the
door. In frustration, Selma hugged herself. She had a headache.

KENAN PACED BACK AND forth in front of Rae's closed bedroom door.
He needed to talk to her and hoped she was still in there. She should have told
him that Selma confronted her, so he could've nipped that in the bud earlier.
Why was Rae keeping secrets?

He slapped his forehead in anger, then slid down the dark brown door,
landing on his butt. What came over him in the bathroom? He wasn't some

sadistic guy. Why did he treat Selma like that? Now, she hated him, and he couldn't blame her.

Kenan watched the bedroom door across the hall. He hoped Selma was okay. He'd never forgive himself if something terrible happened to her now.

He tapped on his sister's door in a slow, steady motion.

"Who is it?" she asked.

Kenan grinned. "Your favorite brother."

Rae opened the door and looked down at him, smiling. "You mean my only brother."

"Same difference." He stood and didn't wait for an invitation to come inside. He scanned the room before sitting on the bed. "Who's in here with you?"

"Just me."

"Rae!" He raised his hands in frustration.

"What? I needed a shower, and it's not like that's a group activity." Rae stood by the dresser; she lowered her eyes. "I heard you and Selma."

Kenan sighed. "Why didn't you tell me she accused you?"

"It literally just happened." Rae gulped when her brother looked at her like that wasn't a valid excuse. "I blamed her too."

"Why?"

She bit her lower lip. "I don't know."

Kenan walked over to Rae. "No, don't do that. Talk to me."

"When we got here, Marissa told me she had invited Adam to make someone jealous. I mean, the only guy I can think to fit the profile is you, so maybe Selma snapped out of jealousy. You were alone with Mar, Kenan. She could've gone out to the lake when you left. You know you're a heavy sleeper."

It seemed no one thought Adam murdered Marissa. They'd rather blame someone they knew than a total stranger. It would make sense for Rae to think his ex still had feelings for Kenan, but Marissa hadn't. At least, she hadn't acted upon them if she did. Even though Selma acted like split personalities earlier, Kenan didn't think she was a killer. "You didn't hear this because you were outside at the time, but Naomi had told Mar that Brady had a crush on her and was jealous of Adam. She was probably talking about him."

"Does he?"

"What?"

"Have a crush on Mar?"

"He said he didn't, but that's not the point." Rae wasn't jealous, was she? Since when would she care about any skank Brady took an interest? "Nothing happened between you last night, right?"

"He was the perfect gentleman."

Kenan folded his arms across his chest, studying her face. No nervousness. No sweat. No quiver of the upper lip; his sister didn't lie. "He's really digging you, Rae. Listen to me. I want you to stay close to Brady."

Rae shrugged her shoulders. "Why?"

"Because I know he'll take care of you like I would if we ever get separated."

Rae nodded. "Speaking of separation, I should go get help."

"Like hell you are. No one's leaving this cabin by themselves."

"I can handle it; you know I can. Let me get us help."

"No."

"We're running out of time. Mar's corpse is rotting away outside. You know the animals will pick at her. You know it." Rae cried. "She was our friend, Kenan. Please. Let me help her."

Kenan took a step closer and shook his head. "The ranger checks on all the homes. He'll be here. We have to stay together."

She wiped tears from her eyes, looking off to the left. "What if he comes too late?"

"He won't."

"You can't promise that."

"Mar is gone, and we can't change that, but we can protect ourselves." Kenan lowered his head. "May she rest in peace; she's in a much better place than we are."

"She was too young to die," Rae whispered. Kenan looked up to make eye contact with her.

There was a time when she didn't think dying in your twenties was too young. There was a time when she'd welcome death with open arms, being jealous of who passed away before she did. But Kenan wouldn't bring it up; he didn't want to upset Rae. Not now anyway, but sooner or later, she would have to face reality.

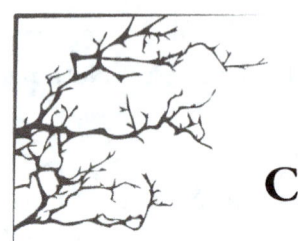

# Chapter Twenty-One

Tobey and the rest of the group, minus Rae and Kenan, huddled in the living room, panic in their eyes. Tobey sat in a chair while Naomi was on his lap. Selma and Logan stood near Adam, and Brady stood by the front door.

"What do you mean there's no rope?" Selma asked.

"I couldn't find any." Tobey patted Naomi's knee.

"What do we do now?" Logan asked.

Kenan and Rae walked downstairs. He entered the living room as she stayed in the entranceway of the kitchen. "What's wrong?" Kenan asked.

Again, Tobey explained how he couldn't find rope in the shed.

Kenan rubbed his forehead. "We can take shifts watching over Adam, or...we can let him go. Doesn't matter what he does, but he wouldn't be staying here."

Adam became wide-eyed. "No, I wouldn't survive out there."

"Should have thought about that before you killed Marissa, you prick." Logan made his way to stand beside Rae.

"You survived last night; you can do it again," Brady said.

"Why should we let him go?" Tobey asked. What was Kenan thinking? Who knew what kind of plotting and traps Adam could create on his own accord, he reasoned.

They didn't need that mystery creeping up on them.

"Because he may not have done it," Selma chimed in.

Adam sighed in relief. "Finally someone believes me."

Selma looked at Adam. "Don't get too excited. You're not completely off the hook." She pointed towards the crowd. "If Adam didn't do it, then one of us did, and I know I didn't kill Marissa, nor damage the Jeeps."

The others chimed in with their I-didn't-do-it-either stances. Before long, everyone yelled over top of one another, trying to get their point across, ultimately not being heard at all. Tobey and Kenan looked at each other. When would the madness stop?

"Shut up," Kenan screamed. Everyone obeyed and gawked at him. "The ranger should get here to check our place by tomorrow night, then we're outta here. Do you guys wanna take shifts watching over Adam, or do you want to let him go? He could fend for himself, and the cops could search for him themselves."

"All this having to look after him will be a waste if he just hires a good attorney to get him off. He's probably a rich bastard, who will bribe himself off. I say let him suffer in the woods alone; that will probably be the only punishment he ever comes across," Brady encouraged.

A couple nodded, and a few shook their heads. Were they really going to play it as a democracy or a dictatorship? If democracy, they could be there all night, trying to reach a decisive vote. Adam was the loudest naysayer about not being kicked out of the cabin. That he'd gladly be watched over, that he wouldn't try to run away.

"It doesn't really sound like a suitable punishment if Adam is volunteering," Naomi said.

"Good point. I say we kick him out," Tobey agreed with his girlfriend. He wanted to support her in any way that he could.

"I say vote him out too. In my heart, I believe he killed Marissa, and I'll be damned if he kills another one of us. Kick his ass out while we're safe locked in the cabin." Logan threw Adam a set of car keys. "You can even stay in the Jeep if you want. Homeboy Brady won't mind sleeping in here now."

"Less stress if Adam isn't in here, but what if that's what the killer wants? What if she wants a person out, who can help fight her off?" Selma placed her hands on her hips.

Kenan rolled his eyes. "I told you to leave her out of it." He stepped toward his girlfriend.

In a bold manner, Selma stood on the couch to grab everyone's attention. "I know what I saw and heard. While the boys were out searching for Marissa, Rae was in here predicting that she was already dead. That was no prediction. That was no feeling. That was an admission of guilt if you ask me." Selma pointed to Rae, so everyone turned to look at her. "Clearly she has issues. Ever since she's stepped foot in here, she's been acting strange. Look at her, she won't even come into the living room." She gave Rae a challenging look. "Why is that? Is that your trigger that makes you snap?"

Kenan grabbed Selma by the arm, forcing her to climb down. He dragged her to the door. "Don't feel safe here, then you can stay outside with Adam."

"I'm safe as long as I don't leave the living room. Or is it you, Kenan? It's your cabin." Selma pouted. "Maybe you and Rae got together to plan ending peoples' lives because you're both sick and twisted due to the ten-year anniversary. Maybe you both invented this RL guy as a cover story."

Tobey lifted Naomi off his lap and walked over to the feuding couple. He tapped Kenan on the shoulder. "Let her go, man." His friend's grip became tighter as he stared at Selma. She didn't back down. If looks could kill. "Come on, let her go. Don't feed into her drama, that's what she wants."

"But she's accusing Rae."

"Let her do whatever she wants. No one believes her. We know you and Rae aren't the killers. It's Adam, and that's the theory I'm sticking to. Forcing Selma outside with him will only get her killed too. I know you don't want that." Tobey pried Kenan's hands off his girlfriend's arm.

Kenan looked at him. "Then you deal with Sel. I can't stand to be around her."

"Ditto." Selma's creeks flushed angry red. "You don't believe me, Tobey. Well, good luck because she's gonna kill us one by one."

"If you really think that, then kill me." Rae stepped forward, pushing out her chest, raising her fists. "Kill me right now."

"Come in here, and I just might," Selma threatened.

Kenan lunged after her again, but Tobey stood in his way. "Selma, if you threaten any of us again, you're outta here, so I suggest you go sit in a corner and shut up," Tobey said.

Selma stuck out her tongue, raised both hands in surrender, and walked over to the couch. She plopped down into it, sinking further and further into the cushions.

How did it turn from Adam killed Marissa, to now it was Rae and maybe Kenan?

"Before you kick me out, can I shower first? Brush my teeth? Possibly eat too?" Adam asked.

Really? He must be truly certifiable; he's accused of killing someone, about to be stranded in a place he has nowhere to turn to, the nearest place like thirty miles. Good luck if he could hike that, and all he could think about was taking a shower. What kind of person was Adam? Were they dealing with floor level six crazy? Or floor level seven?

"Hell naw. This ain't the Holiday Inn, pretty boy." Brady gave Adam an icy stare. Adam gave one right back.

"Wait. I have an idea." Rae ran upstairs with Kenan following her. They came back minutes later with a bunch of clothes.

Selma squinted her eyes. "This isn't a shopping spree."

"Adam doesn't want to be kicked out, and it may not be safe to have him around. We'll tie him up with these clothes. Win-win."

"THANKS FOR HAVING MY back earlier. Now if only you could convince them to let me shower, eat, and brush my teeth," Adam joked. Even though he was tied up, it still felt good that some people believed him. It was probably the only thing keeping him alive, he thought.

"I didn't do it for you." Rae glanced around the empty living room. Everyone else had scattered into different groups. Some left through the back entrance of the kitchen, and some went upstairs.

If only he could get inside her head. "Why don't you come in the living room?" Maybe Selma had a point earlier.

"I'm good."

"That doesn't answer my question." Adam smiled. If he were going to win her over, then he'd have to use his charms and good looks. Good thing Rae was single.

"Why did you kill Marissa?"

"I didn't. You know how it feels to be wrongly accused. Your brother took it harder than you."

Rae shrugged. "I know I didn't do it. That's all that matters."

"If only it was that simple. I know I didn't do it, and here I am tied up, hoping no one gets revenge."

"Just earlier you thanked me; I guess that was a lie."

She was more conniving than Adam thought. Rae would probably give him a run for his money. She was good at twisting words.

"I'm definitely grateful to be here instead of outside."

Kenan strolled through the front door and made his way to stand near his sister. "I thought you were upstairs with Tobey, Selma, and Naomi."

"I never said I was."

Kenan grabbed her wrist. "What are you thinking being alone with him?"

"Someone needs to keep an eye on him." She wiggled out of his grasp.

"Not you. A guy. Go ahead. I'll look after him."

"No, I don't mind."

He rolled his eyes. "Rae."

She put her hands on her hips. "Kenan."

Adam thought Selma and Naomi had feistiness, but he shouldn't have underestimated the wallflower. Looked like Rae didn't need much protection. He smirked at them bickering.

Kenan stood in front of her, blocking her view of Adam. He hovered over her. "He killed Mar."

"Allegedly." Adam raised a finger as if making a point in a classroom lecture. "I allegedly killed Marissa. What ever happened to innocent until proven guilty?"

Without turning around, Kenan said, "Now you know how a black man feels when he goes up against a judge and jury."

"I'm half-black. My mom is black and my dad is Hawaiian," Adam lied.

Kenan laughed. "So you're one of us? Yeah right."

"I swear." Adam pointed out celebrities who were half-black but didn't look like it.

Kenan shook his head in disappointment. "Then this sucks even more that you're making another brother end up in prison."

Adam stared at Rae when Kenan shifted his body. It seemed like she never took her eyes off of Adam as if she was trying to read his mind or something. Maybe there was something freaky about her. Selma had said something about Rae having visions.

"Come on, Rae. He's only going to try and get inside your head," Kenan warned.

She whispered, "Has it ever occurred to you that I'm trying to get inside his head? Trying to get answers? He's more likely to open up to someone he's not scared of. Please Kenan, let me try this."

Kenan sighed. "I'll stay with you."

"No, I have to do this alone. He'll shut down with you around."

"No way."

"Please, Kenan. For Mar."

"Fine, but scream if he tries any funny business."

She sighed in relief. "I promise."

Kenan returned outside through the back door.

"Why don't you come in here?" Adam asked.

"I'm good." Rae smirked. "You stink."

Adam gulped. Way to hit below the belt. "I have a feeling whether I smelled good or not, you still wouldn't come over. Why?"

"Tell me why you killed Marissa, then I'll tell you why I avoid the living room." She folded her arms across her chest.

"Can I trust you?"

Rae nodded.

"No, I need to hear it. Can I trust you?"

"Yes." She leaned closer in anticipation to hear the secret shared between the two of them.

"I was hell bent that I didn't lay a finger on her until your brother said he left me alone with her. Now, I'm not so sure. Maybe I blacked-out because I don't remember anything; I had no idea how I ended up sleeping in that shed last night. That night is a blur. I know I was upset when I saw Brady and Marissa together, but I'm not a violent person...if I did anything, I don't remember. I was blacked-out."

If they were to bond on any level, then she had to trust Adam. He had to be a little honest to get leeway.

"If that's the case and it was a one time thing, then why did you take out the car parts?"

"I don't remember—"

"You were blacked-out," Rae finished his sentence. She took a deep breath, closing her eyes. "So you don't want to kill any of us? You're not some maniac on a killing spree?"

"Hell no." Now it was her turn. Her answer would reveal if Adam got through to her or not. "What's up with you and the living room?"

"You sound like a broken record, do you know that?" She sighed and fidgeted with her fingers. Rae lowered her gaze to the wooden floor. "Something terrible happened and whenever I step foot in there, those horrid memories come flashing back. Even seeing you tied up like that reminds me of what Kenan and I went through ten years ago...I guess since I didn't get to ask my parents' killers any questions, I'm doing it through you." Rae raised her head slowly to make eye contact with Adam. She brushed her cheek with the palm of her hand and swiped tears away.

Adam's tear strolled down his cheek. Man that was deep. She'd do anything to get answers from him, so she would keep him alive. Kenan seemed to listen to her, so maybe Adam would survive this after all. Unless she was lying and playing him. Something told him that Rae was serious and felt relief getting that off her chest though.

"Your secret is safe with me," Adam promised.

A weak smile formed on Rae's lips. "Thank you." He saw the wheels turning in her head. "Hey, what did you mean by you saw Brady and Marissa together?"

"When you guys left to get food, I wanted to clean up, but I felt bad for leaving her with Brady. When I reached them, I hid behind a tree. It's not like I could interrupt what they were doing." Rae's brown eyes widened; he definitely had her attention now. "They were hooking up. You know, having sex out in the open."

"Brady and Marissa," she whispered.

"Yep, and I accused him in front of everyone while you were outside, but he denied it all. He's a fucking liar." Adam scooted up in the chair to be a little closer to Rae. "Don't trust him, Rae. He fucked Marissa then probably killed her."

Adam couldn't tell if she believed him or not because she produced a poker face to the news. Had something been going on with Rae and Brady? Did he sneak behind her back?

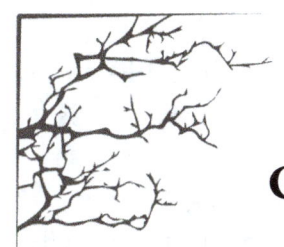

# Chapter Twenty-Two

Naomi examined the back of Selma's head. She felt the bump that expand-ed past Selma's hair. "Does that hurt?" she asked.

Selma flinched. "A little." Tobey, who appeared doubtful, caught her atten-tion. She had just finished telling them how Kenan had gotten violent with her, even spitting at her three times. Selma had to lie; the more she made Kenan seem unstable, the more eyes would be watching him.

If the real killer thought everyone paid attention to Adam or Kenan, then they'd get comfortable and slip up somewhere. Selma was determined to solve the mystery by any means necessary.

"I honestly think Rae has something to do with this," Selma continued while Naomi shook her head. "Before you shut me down, just listen. She never wanted to come to this cabin in the first place. It's probably like a big fuck you to everyone for making her re-live her pain." She focused her attention on To-bey. "Think about it. She left last night without anyone noticing. She could've gone to the lake, killed Marissa, and then slept with Brady in the Jeep. Who knows? Maybe she and Kenan are in on it? They know their way around the woods." Selma looked at Naomi. "How can someone sleep through someone damaging the Jeeps? It's not like popping the hood is a quiet thing. It's loud and shakes the vehicle. No way anyone sleeps through that, so maybe Brady's in on it too."

"Adam wants us to turn on each other, and you're feeding right into his trap," Tobey said.

Selma rolled her eyes. "Not you guys too. Open your eyes or you'll get killed like Marissa."

"No, listen to yourself. You've managed to blame over half of us. At this rate, everyone had their part." Tobey rolled his eyes and frowned. "I know you're mad at Kenan, but it doesn't mean you should make his or Rae's life a liv-ing hell right now. They've been through so much."

Selma shook her head. "How long can that be an excuse for them?"

Naomi and Tobey shared a look. "It's not an excuse. It's the truth," Naomi said. She held her boyfriend's hand as if they were a joint entity, like Selma wouldn't be able to break them.

"Good thing you're on their side. Maybe now Kenan won't get violent with you." Selma stormed out of the room. She was dealing with idiots, she scolded herself.

She entered her own room—Kenan better sleep somewhere else—slammed the door, and locked it. She should have taken Rae up on her offer to take the knife as a weapon. Had Rae told anyone about their secret? Hopefully, she'd keep her mouth shut.

Selma only needed to test Adam, Logan, and Brady to see what they knew. If she got enough accounts, then she could piece the puzzle together. Apparently, she'd have to do it alone unless Logan and Brady came to their senses. She'd have to be careful with Adam due to his desperation.

She lay on her back. She closed her eyes and fell asleep.

TOBEY SHOOK HIS HEAD. "See, I told you we should stick together. Otherwise, you'll be sounding ridiculous like Selma."

"You don't think there's any truth in what she said? Not even a possibility?"

He sat up in bed then leaned sideways to face Naomi, who lay comfortably on her side. "I thought we already went through this in the shed. Adam did it. Case closed."

Naomi knew that Tobey was right, deep down, but she also understood how Selma felt. No one but Naomi and she were around when Rae rambled on and on about knowing Marissa was dead. She did sound like a lunatic, however, Naomi knew her best friend wasn't a killer, even when Rae went on and on about knowing they're all doomed.

Tobey rubbed her leg. "Omi, did you hear me?"

"Yeah, baby. I get your point."

"You seem so down; you should go tanning. That always cheers you up."

"Tanning where?"

"At the lake."

"I can never go back there, and it's not like I can go lay out on the porch. Marisa's there, rotting away." Naomi covered her mouth. "I'm sorry. You know what I mean."

"I want you to relax."

"How? Everything's gone wrong this weekend. People are turning on each other; I can't handle the stress. If you weren't here, I don't know what I'd do."

"You have me, Omi. Always. I love you, and if I could take your pain away, I would."

Naomi smiled weakly. "I love you too...you should talk to your boy. Violence isn't cool."

"I'll talk to him, but I really don't think he did what she said."

"You think she caused that lump on her head by herself?"

Tobey shrugged. "Something may have happened, but I think she exaggerated to make sure we were on her side. Not to sound sexist but beware of a woman scorned. Revenge outweighs common sense in that scenario every time."

Naomi playfully slapped Tobey on the arm. "*Anyways*, thank you for trying to make me feel better. Just being here helps a lot."

"I still wish you'd do your favorite thing. You sure you don't want to tan? It's not like you'll get in the water."

Yawning, she shook her head. "It wouldn't feel right."

"Then take a nap. Maybe you'll feel better once you wake up."

She nodded. It had been a long day; she could use some relaxation and escape for a little while. Hopefully, she'd have pleasant dreams. Please no nightmares, she wished. Naomi closed her eyes, almost drifting to sleep to the point she barely felt Tobey's tender kiss on her lips. She didn't respond to his plea of making sure she locked the door, so she wouldn't be disturbed. Her body was comfortable to the point she couldn't get up.

She'd just have to take her chances of possibly being awakened.

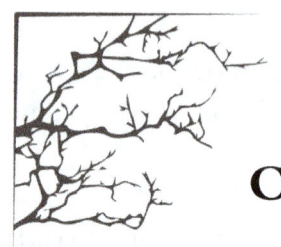

# Chapter Twenty-Three

Tobey stumbled upon Kenan and Rae near Adam. He snuck up behind Rae and put his arm around her shoulders. "I'm sorry for what Selma said earlier; don't worry. No one will turn against you, no matter how hard she tries."

"Thank you, Tobey." She smiled.

He squeezed his grip, then let go. He focused his attention on Kenan. "Is Adam acting up?"

"Nah, Rae insists on keeping him company, so I decided to be the third wheel."

Rae rolled her eyes. "The uninvited third wheel."

Kenan stuck out his tongue. "Where's Naomi?"

"Taking a nap," Tobey answered.

"And *Selma*?"

Probably no love lost there, Tobey assumed. "Upstairs I think. She left our room in a huff, then I heard a door slam. I'm assuming that was her."

"Yes, her famous tempter tantrums." Kenan pouted. "What happened?"

"You know, same ole, same ole. Basically, what she had said downstairs. I guess she thought we're deaf."

"I don't trust Selma upstairs with Naomi," Rae said.

"Why?" What happened between Rae, Selma, and Kenan? They acted as if they were partaking in a centuries old feud instead of a one day thing, heck, hadn't even been twenty-four hours yet.

"She thinks Selma was jealous that I spent alone time with Marissa and probably killed her," Kenan answered for his sister. Did everyone have their own wacked out theories?

"Really? You think Selma is capable of murder?"

"I know it seems like I'm retaliating because she accused me, but I'm not. I have my reasons, but I don't think she took the belts. So either it's not her. Period. Or she's working with someone." Rae looked at Adam. "Or if he did it, he was blacked-out and doesn't remember."

"How convenient." Kenan slapped Adam in the back of the head—Gibb's style.

Adam flinched. "It's the truth, bro."

"I can't stand to look at him; let's go outside. Naomi's not after Kenan, so she should be safe." Tobey chuckled, putting his arm around Rae again. "Come on, before he gets inside your head. He wants us to turn on each other." He led them to the door.

"I'll be out. I just have to tighten the clothes some more." Kenan meddled with the back of Adam's chair. Rae placed her hand on the doorknob.

Brady and Logan were chilling on the back porch. How anyone could act as if their surroundings were normal with a dead body under a blanket was beyond Tobey. But there they were, sitting in rocking chairs.

Logan shot up from his seat. "Here Rae, you can sit here."

Brady smirked. "After he's farted three times in the seat. Guess to keep you warm."

Logan's cheeks turned red. "He's lying." He eyed Brady. "Why don't you stop acting like a child?"

"Oh please, get off your high horse. We're men; that's what we do. We act like horny, stupid teenagers and hope that a wonderful girl like Rae accepts us for who we are." Brady winked at her.

"I'm good," Rae declined to sit, causing Brady to chuckle.

Apparently, she wasn't okay because she kept staring at the blanket as though she was trying to get it to disappear. "You okay, Rae?" Tobey asked.

While the other guys thought with their dicks, he would think with his heart and be a good friend. He'd comfort his best friend's sister with no strings attached.

Before she could answer, Kenan stepped outside, closing the door. Logan sat back down in his seat; he watched Rae's movements, so did Brady. Was it concern, or did they consider what Selma said?

"What do you guys think about me going for help instead of waiting on the ranger?" Rae asked.

"Rae!" Kenan scolded.

She glared at her brother with determined eyes. "*Or* Kenan can go. *Or* we can go together while you guys wait here."

Kenan shook his head repeatedly. "It's not safe."

'It's a better option than staying here with a killer."

"No, and that's final. Rae, if I have to tie you up beside your best friend, then I will to keep you here."

Logan shifted forward in his chair. "Best friend?"

"She was bonding with Adam and cocked an attitude because I interrupted." Kenan raised his hands in mock surrender. "My bad."

Rae put her hands on both hips. "What's your problem?"

"What's my problem? What's my problem? I'm freaking out; that's my problem. But I can't, I have to protect you."

"I didn't ask for your help!"

"You don't have to ask for it! Ever Rae! I'll always be there for you!" Kenan took a step closer to her, so Tobey jumped in between them. "When I say something, it's in your best interest. Please stop fighting me on this."

Rae began to cry. "I want to go home."

"We'll get there tomorrow night unless RL stops by." Kenan's voice softened. "I promise you, Rae."

RAE PARKED HERSELF on top of the porch step with her back facing the boys. She tuned them out, especially her brother. She was thankful that he was there for her, but he was suffocating her. It made her feel like a child in front of their friends.

Rae sighed.

Birds chirped and hawked in the distance. A group of them, maybe vultures, circled the sky. Rae glanced at the blanket. Those damn birds could probably smell Marissa, and the second everyone left, they'd pounce on her. Rae needed to guard her best friend's body if there was any hope for an open casket.

Logan bumped into her. "What you thinking about?"

When did he sit there? Had he been by her side the entire time? Rae shrugged.

Instead of letting the silence speak for itself, he pried more. "You can talk to me, Rae. Is it about Kenan?"

Kenan. He was acting different, way more over-productive than usual, ever since they arrived in Virginia. The stress was getting to her brother; there was no denying that.

It dawned on her that she couldn't hear any voices. She rotated the upper part of her body. "Where did everyone go?"

"They left. You didn't notice? They said 'see ya later' and everything."

Rae gave Logan a questioned look. Was she in such a daze that she wasn't even paying attention to people anymore? Besides worrying about Kenan, she should worry about herself too. "I didn't hear them."

"Are you okay, Rae?"

No, but it wasn't as if she could say that. Kenan would be on her like red on blood. "There's a lot on my mind."

"You should let people in to relieve some of that pain. When I say people, I don't mean Adam."

"Are you okay, Logan? Have you talked to anyone about what's been happening?" How did it feel to be treated like he'll break in a second? To be treated like he was a depressed, sad sack of a human?

He hesitated, blinked rapidly, and wiped sweat from his forehead. "Actually, I haven't really. There's so much I'd like to say to you, but I don't know why I haven't. I mean a lot has happened, yeah, but all the misery has taught me life's too short to not take risks."

What did he want to tell her? The way he seemed, it was really personal and important. Her heart beat quickened. Was he going to say he had feelings for her?

"What risks would you take?" she asked.

"To kiss you," Logan whispered.

Rae blushed. "Really? Since when?"

"Since we first met."

She reached over and stroked his hand. "You have no idea how much that means to me. I would like you to kiss me." They gazed into each other's eyes, not daring to lean over for a kiss in case Kenan walked on the porch again.

They had held onto temptation for so many years that a little longer wouldn't hurt.

"You have no idea how much that means to me..." He lowered his eyes. "I thought maybe you liked Brady."

"We're just friends."

"Which is usually code for friends with benefits."

Rae shook her head. She removed her hand from Logan's touch. "I'm not into codes. What you see is what you get with me." She wanted to change the subject and get his opinion. "Did it sink in what Selma said? Do you think I killed Marissa?" She looked over at the blanket and sighed. What if he said yes? You could have a crush on someone, but still be suspicious of them.

"Of course you didn't. She was your best friend, besides you have a good heart. You couldn't hurt a fly."

"So you don't think me and Kenan are in on some elaborate plan to kill all of you?"

Logan shook his head. "Hell naw."

"Not even a possibility?"

He laughed. "You worry too much, Rae. We all have your back and your brother's back. Selma won't change that."

They smiled at each other. He tucked a strand of hair behind Rae's ear. Maybe Logan would kiss her after all. At this point, Kenan would just have to get over it and be happy for the both of them.

Out of nowhere, a loud, screeching scream assaulted their earlobes, making the hair rise on both of their necks.

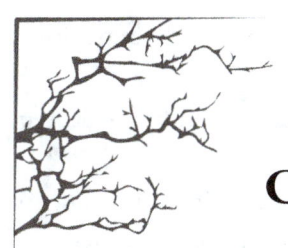

# Chapter Twenty-Four

The screeching was coming from Selma, and she couldn't stop once she saw Naomi's blood splattered over the cover and sheet set. The pillow was soaked, dark red. A trail of blood led onto the floor, probably leaving a stain forever. The sight would no doubtedly torture her dreams, haunt her memories, and torture her psyche.

It appeared as though Naomi was the unfortunate victim of a psychotic butcher. Her throat was deeply slashed. She was carved open from chest to stomach, her organs spilled out, looking like sausages stuffed in casings. She resembled a whitetail deer that a hunter just bagged and then gutted.

But what really freaked out Selma was that Naomi's eyeballs were chiseled out of her sockets, so only now deep black holes were present. The sick bastard shoved her eyeballs inside her wide-opened mouth. On her face, two slits were etched on her cheeks to give the expression of a sinister grin. The knife was placed beside Naomi's body.

Kenan, who had been standing by Selma, held her when she collapsed in his arms.

Tobey ran into the room followed by Brady. Wide-eyed, Brady vomited on the floor. Tobey's eyes bulged as his mouth fell open at the sight. "Is that...Is that...No! Oh no! That's...my Omi!" In a rage, he turned and yelled at Selma. "My God! What the fuck did you do?"

"I found her. I didn't kill her," Selma managed to say between sobs.

Tobey gave her the evil eye. "I'll fucking kill you!"

"I didn't do it!" Selma argued back, covering her face with her hands.

Of course, she looked suspicious. How could she explain that she didn't hear anything? That she had slept through it? Selma's body convulsed, thinking if it hadn't been Naomi, then it could have been her. She'd never be alone again. That's if the group would let her stay with them. What if they tied her up like Adam?

Tobey sobbed. His body quivered as he fell to the floor. Brady bent down to wrap his arms around him.

Footsteps hurried up the stairs. "Logan, don't let Rae come in here!" Kenan screamed.

Brady shut the door in Logan's face. Someone kept knocking loudly, probably stubborn Rae. Brady went back to holding Tobey. "I locked it in case they tried to come in. Sorry, I panicked. Should I open the door? What should I do?"

"Keep it locked. Rae can't see this," Kenan said in between sniffs. His grip didn't loosen up on Selma. There was no way she could deal with the image of Naomi's dead body. She'd need Kenan. Maybe he'd need her too.

"Omi. My baby, my baby," Tobey whispered to no one in particular. Poor Tobey. He shouldn't be in the room. In fact, no one should witness this. No one could deal.

"Did you hear anything?" Kenan asked.

"No, I was asleep." Selma blaming Rae earlier would backfire in her face. She was the one found near Naomi's body and hadn't heard anything. Even that sounded shady to Selma.

Oh, shit. She was in trouble if the group turned on her. Would that be her karma if they did?

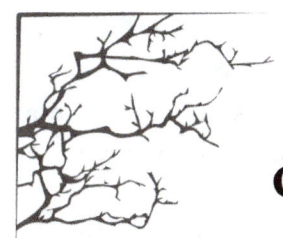

# Chapter Twenty-Five

Adam stood in front of the mirror that was fogged by the steam from his hot shower. Sweat seeped through his body, soaking his gray v-neck and navy blue skinny jeans. In nervousness, his eyes—adjusted to the pitch dark—shifted to the lock door.

It was a good idea at the time to get loose and wander off alone. Some people thought he was innocent, so their conscience wouldn't allow him to die from revenge. At the worst, they'd kick him out, but Adam would just sleep in the Jeep for a night. If Brady and Rae handled it, then he could too. Now, he regretted that decision because he could hear the ruckus across the hall.

If something happened again, they'd blame 'the stranger.'

Adam prayed that no one would find him. He stood still, as quiet as possible. He held his breath in fear of deep breathing. How could he get out of this? All he had to do was get through tonight. The ranger would arrive by then; the authorities could do whatever they wanted with him. Brady was right—Adam was rich, and the family lawyer would have the charges dropped instantly. No case. No evidence.

He was afraid to take a step because the floorboards could creak. Why didn't he run away just as a sensible guy would? Damn his obsession with clean hygiene. That one mistake could get Adam murdered. He gulped, then scolded himself for making too much noise.

His stomach growled. Seriously, did it have to do that now? It's not as though Adam hadn't eaten breakfast. Wait, he hadn't. He shook his head in defeat; his body was trying to get him caught.

Sooner or later, they would calm down, unite, and hunt Adam. He needed to get a decent head start. It was time to take a chance on a neighbor, shotgun be damned. It would be best to escape while they were rowdy and preoccupied.

From what? Adam had no clue.

He tiptoed at a turtle's pace towards the door and unbolted it. Adam stopped and waited. Damn that loud clicking sound. Silence came from the hall. They must not have heard him. If he were going to make a run for it, now would be the time. He crept as quietly as possible, damn the creaking, to the locked bedroom door.

Adam counted to ten, breathing slowly, trying to get his heartbeat to calm down. Maybe this would be the biggest mistake of his life. What if they saw him? The voices were literally outside the door. He started to doubt himself.

If he was going to stay in the room to hide, then he needed to unlock the door. Keeping it locked would be a dead giveaway that Adam was hiding in there. Would they even search in the house? Wouldn't they assume he escaped? That's what a normal, rational being would do.

What to do? What to do? Every decision had pros and cons. Adam was anxious to roam the woods alone. He didn't know his way around; plus, it was pretty dark outside. He knew he could not hide in the shed again.

This decision could make or break his life, his limbs. His nose was already broken, causing him to breathe heavily. Could he keep the noise down? If he stayed, maybe Adam could sneak into the kitchen to get something to eat. For now, he'd hide in the closet. That would have to do; it was too risky to attempt anything else.

Adam unclicked the lock then tiptoed into the closet. If the room appeared exactly the same, no one would be suspicious or look around. He bent down and sat on the dusty floor with his knees holding his head up. *Please don't cramp up. Please don't cramp up. Please don't cramp up.* He hoped he made the right decision.

LOGAN SHIVERED. THERE had to be a valid reason why they didn't want him and Rae in that room. With all the commotion, it had to be devastating.

Rae pounded on the door. "Let me in! Let me in!" He reached for her hand, but she jerked it away.

What if another friend was dead? No, it couldn't be. Maybe someone got really hurt, and blood gushed everywhere. Kenan, Selma, and Brady's voices echoed through the thin wall. Where were Tobey and Naomi?

"Get Rae away from the door!" Kenan yelled.

Rae squinted her eyes. "Let me in!"

"Get her the fuck away from the door!"

Logan gulped. His friend had urgency and desperation in his voice like it was an emergency. What if it was more than someone got hurt? He touched Rae's back. "Maybe we should leave and give them space."

"I'm not leaving until someone tells me what's going on! Let me in!" Rae didn't even look in his direction, leaning into the door.

"They're not going to open it. You screaming and banging isn't helping. Let's walk away, then they'll fill us in when they get out," he encouraged. Maybe if Logan was calm, he could rub that off on Rae.

She kicked the door out of frustration. Logan understood her temperament but having outbursts wasn't productive. Who knew—maybe Rae's reaction was the normal one?

Why was he composed? Something bad happened. Maybe Selma cracked, seizing one of the guys at knifepoint. Logan was afraid to know what happened in that room. If he wasn't informed, he could stay in denial, stay in the dark. If told, Logan would have to face the problem head-on.

Why couldn't things be stress free until the ranger arrived?

"I swear to God, get her away from the fucking door! Drag her ass if you have to. She can't see this!" Kenan yelled again.

Rae couldn't see it, but could Logan handle it? He doubted it. He touched her back again. "Let's go, Rae."

"Why won't they let me in? I have a right to know what's going on." She sounded defeated. "Please let me in."

Logan's heart sank.

Instead of sharing butterflies in their stomach or acting like teens falling in love for the first time, Rae and Logan were afraid for their lives, afraid for their safety, not knowing if they or their friends would survive this weekend.

Since she was weeping, it was effortless leading her away. If he could relieve her pain and suffering, then he would with no hesitation. Rae fell into his arms; Logan led her to the stairs. They sat down on the top step.

Where were Tobey and Naomi? Keeping an eye on Adam? Maybe the stairs weren't far enough away; it probably taunted Rae. Maybe they should leave. It troubled Logan to think that Adam understood Rae and could get her to calm down. A big possibility. "Let's go downstairs."

Without hesitation, she rose, waiting for Logan to lead the way. They locked arms and went down the steps slowly as if they were old and may break a hip. At the kitchen table, he pulled out a chair, so she could sit down. "Want something to eat or drink?"

She shook her head. "How can you be so laidback? Something happened in that room. Aren't you the least bit curious of what happened?" She studied his reaction.

Logan rubbed the back of his neck. "I'm being strong for the both of us, so I can't freak out."

"I wish you would. That would make me feel a whole lot better if you had my back upstairs. Then maybe they would've opened the door, and we wouldn't be sitting here like clueless owls."

Owls? Logan wanted to laugh about her word choice but thought against it. "I'll always have your back."

"No, you acted like Kenan, bossing me around. He doesn't always know what's best for me, you know."

Logan hung his head down low, looking at the floor. The last thing he wanted was the girl of his dreams to picture him as her brother.

TOBEY EVADED EVERYONE'S gaze. He stood in front of the window in a daze, his back facing the rest of the people in the room, who were by the nightstand. "Please get out and give me a minute. I want to be alone with Omi," he pleaded.

Kenan, Selma, and Brady obeyed. They huddled in the hallway by the door. "Hey Brady, can you stay here for when Tobey comes out? We'll be downstairs," Kenan said.

Brady nodded, unable to speak.

Selma and Kenan found the others sitting at the kitchen table. They held hands. It seemed like Logan did a good job of comforting Rae. Now the hard part: telling Rae her friend died. Not only died but someone tortured her friend like their parents. Not only died and tortured, but it happened right upstairs, in their old bedroom.

Kenan took a deep breath then shared a look with Selma, who hugged herself. How could he break the news? If only she could do it.

As if reading Kenan's mind, Selma whispered, "We have something to tell you. Naomi..." her voice trailed off. She lowered her eyes to the floor.

"Naomi what?" Rae squeezed Logan's hand tighter.

He sauntered over to his sister and bent down to grab her free hand. "Naomi's...Naomi's gone like Marissa."

In an unexpected twist, Rae didn't shatter. She didn't shiver or break into a sweat. She didn't become wide-eyed or have an open mouth expression. She sat like a zombie, staring off into space. Maybe a defense mechanism?

"What do you mean she's gone? She was just hanging out with us a little while ago!" Logan's voice rose higher and higher like an opera singer. Instead of a beautiful melody, it was full of frustration, confusion, and anger.

Kenan hesitated before responding. There wasn't really a way to sugar coat this information. He knew because he had tried to think of something. "In her bed, someone slit her throat."

Selma nudged his arm. "More than that. Tell them, Kenan."

Kenan swallowed a knot in his throat.

Logan and Rae waited impatiently. "Come on, man, what happened? What can be worse than that?" he asked.

Kenan and Selma shared a glance. "She...she was cut."

"Like slices on her body?" Logan rubbed his chin.

"Kenan, tell them." Selma elbowed him again.

Back to reality, Rae rose in a panic. "Please, Kenan, what's going on?"

He took a deep breath, shaking his head. This wouldn't end well, he thought. "Na—Naomi's throat was slit and she...she was gutted limb to limb."

Rae collapsed back into her chair.

Logan stood and covered his mouth. "What the fuck?"

Kenan held his sister tight. "I'm so sorry."

Rae's arms lay lifeless by her side.

Logan paced back and forth. He halted at the entrance near the living room; the bottom of his sneakers screeched along the wooden floor. "Where's Adam?"

Selma ran over to him. "What?"

"Where's Adam?" Logan repeated.

Kenan rubbed Rae's back; he wanted to go over to see what they were talking about, but couldn't abandon her like this. She'd probably never be the same again. Just hearing the word 'gutted' probably took an emotional toll on her, probably crippled her soul.

Logan and Selma entered the other room. Kenan looked at his sister. "Can you get up? Or do you want to stay here?"

"I can get up." She sniffed, stood, then followed Kenan into the living room, not hesitating or anything. He didn't know what Selma meant by Rae had issues—another exaggeration from Ms. Drama Queen.

The chair was empty; the clothes that held Adam captive lay on the floor. Kenan rubbed his forehead. "When did he escape?"

"I'm going to kill that motherfucker! Torturing women!" Logan spun in circles. "Why doesn't he try that mess on a real man? Because he knows he'd get slaughtered!"

Kenan held his sister's arm for support, backing them away. Rae got out of his grip and walked towards Logan. Maybe to try and calm him down?

Seconds later, the window shattered. Logan's brains splattered on Rae before he dropped to the floor, an arrow stuck through his forehead.

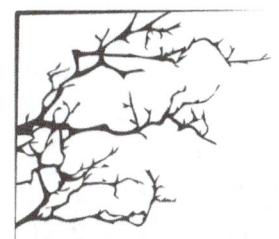

# Chapter Twenty-Six

Was that glass? What happened downstairs? Brady ran to check. He figured it was okay to desert Tobey; only crying echoed through the walls. There wasn't much he could do with the locked door as a barricade.

No one in the kitchen, everything in place. In the living room, Kenan, Selma, and Rae stretched out on their stomachs, shielding their heads with their arms and hands. "What's going on?" Brady asked.

"Get down," Kenan whispered.

He didn't hesitate when he spotted Logan dead on the floor, glass near the window. They waited what felt like an eternity for any kind of noise outside to indicate that the killer was still out there. "We can't stay here."

"Brady's right," Selma yelled.

"Keep your voice down." Kenan took a deep breath, keeping his eye on the front door. "Okay listen, we're crawling ourselves out of here. Me and Selma will look for Tobey. Brady, please help Rae get cleaned up."

Rae cleaned up? Please God don't let her be wounded. Brady peered in her direction; red chunks dyed her hair. Her head was buried onto the floorboards as though she was afraid to look up. What if she was decorated with Logan's blood and guts? That had to take an emotional toll. Could she even function?

Brady lay still while Kenan and Selma slinked past him. Rae didn't budge. The others rummaged through the kitchen, opening cabinets and getting frustrated with finding nothing.

"Rae?" He made sure to keep his voice low.

She didn't acknowledge his presence, so he slid his body like a worm over to her. He patted her hand. "Rae, we have to go. It's not safe down here."

"What's the point? It's safe nowhere; we're gonna die, Brady."

"I won't let anything happen to you."

"You can't promise that."

"Please, Rae. Don't give up. It's a group versus one."

"Then why does the killer keep winning?"

"Please, Rae, come with me. We'll talk while we get you cleaned up. Please."

"There's no point."

"Come on, or I'll drag you upstairs. Either way you're coming with me."

Rae lifted her head, and Brady involuntary threw up. Pieces of brain and blood oozed down her face. She looked like a zombie who had just finished a human meal.

Brady's cheeks turned red. How could she see him as a protector if he vomited all over the place? No wonder Rae gave up.

She proceeded to stand.

"No crawl," Brady said with urgency in his voice. They crept to the stairs, passing the other survivors, and went upstairs on their hands and knees.

They made their way to Brady and Logan's room. Brady bolted the door because they couldn't be too careful. Then they proceeded to the bathroom, once again locking the door. It'd be much safer there—no windows.

Rae stood at the sink to wash her face with soap. She hadn't waited for Brady to hand her a washcloth, instead she used it as a towel. He gargled with mouth rinse and spat in the toilet, which reminded him of earlier. He covered his mouth, fighting the urge to throw up again.

A weak smile formed on Rae's lips. "Are you pregnant?"

"Haha, very funny."

"Might as well have fun before we die. I even cleaned myself, so you wouldn't get sick again."

How thoughtful. Brady was bummed that he missed the opportunity to have that special moment with Rae, taking care of her, wiping her down. He focused on her cleavage. Right dab in the middle of her bra was a red chunk of Logan's gore. "Missed a spot."

Rae lowered her sight to the spot where Brady stared. She frowned, picked up the nasty thing, and flung it in the sink. It made a thud sound. She took her shirt off, tossed it on the sink, then plucked chunks out of her hair. Rae seemed oblivious, standing only in a bra in front of Brady.

He was only human, so of course, he got an erection. Embarrassed, he spun around. In better circumstances, he would have made a move on her, but not like this. If only she knew how much she affected him. He stripped off his long sleeve shirt and passed it backwards to Rae. "Here you go. Wear this."

"Thanks."

Brady tugged at his wife beater and wiped sweat off his forehead. He may die at any second, yet all he could think about was sex. He was a horny guy; he couldn't help it.

Sex was probably the furthest from Rae's mind. She hadn't even bothered asking why his back faced her. Maybe she already knew.

*Think about baseball. Think about grandma. Think about anything except Rae's banging body.* Imagining grandma helped. Brady sighed in relief and turned to face Rae. "Where's Adam?"

She shrugged her shoulders. "He was gone. Maybe the killer took him."

"It's him. It has to be him."

"Where would he gave gotten all these weapons? It's not him. It's killers outside our group. They'll torture us. I can't go through this again." Rae's voice trailed off through her sobs.

Brady walked over to her and wiped her tears. "I can't even imagine what you must be going through right now, but I promise I'll get you out alive."

"Don't say that. Please don't say that. We're all being wiped out right after each other. I can't take anymore." She fell into the sink. "Please, Brady, I can't lose you too. I can't lose anyone else."

He enveloped his arms around her; she placed her head on his chest. If only there wasn't a mystery surrounding this killer, then they'd have a chance of out-smarting him. Of winning. "You won't lose me, Rae."

"You can't promise that."

Brady couldn't promise, but he'd try his darnedest to make that statement true. Would that be enough?

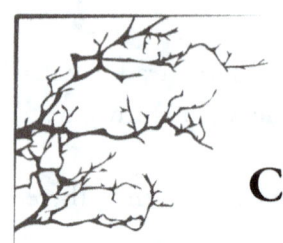

# Chapter Twenty-Seven

Selma searched in the den. She slammed the cabinet. "How the hell is there nothing in this God forsaken place? No guns! No nothing! How can we protect ourselves? Huh! How—"

Kenan grabbed her arm, turning her around. "Selma, calm down."

"We can't stop looking! He's gonna kill us!"

"Keep your voice down, or he may find us."

Selma knew he was right, but she was in panic mode. She didn't want to die. Whom to trust? Did she even have that much time to decide? The killer was wiping them off like a *Call of Duty* game, except this wasn't a game where you could renew lives after hitting the restart button. This was real life. "We have to get out of here."

"I know. It's not safe to spend the night. We'll have to walk out of here."

Selma nodded. "I'm sorry for accusing you and Rae."

Kenan caressed her cheek. "You should tell her that."

"All hope isn't lost." She rushed upstairs, tailed by Kenan. She shook the doorknob on Tobey's door, but it was locked. She banged on it. "Tobey, let us in."

Within minutes, a grief-stricken Tobey answered the door. No time for condolences or to see if he was okay; she needed that knife placed on the bed. She grabbed it.

Kenan jumped. "Hey be careful."

"I got this. We need to find Rae and Brady, then get the fuck out of here." Selma marched over to Rae's room. The door was open with no one inside. She took off for Marissa's room—empty. She tried to open Brady's door, but it was locked. She pounded on it. "Let me in!"

Before long, Brady opened it, ushered everyone in, peeked in the hallway, then quickly shut and locked the door behind them.

"No time for locked doors. We have to get out of here," Selma demanded. "Where's Rae?"

"I'm here." Rae walked out of the bathroom. She gasped, staring at the bloody knife. "Is that—"

"Yes, it killed Naomi; now, we'll use it on the murderer," Selma answered.

Rae covered her mouth, and Brady wrapped his arms around her.

"What's going on?" Tobey asked.

"Logan's dead," Kenan said.

Tobey's eyes widened. "What?"

"It just happened. We were downstairs. Adam's gone, and an arrow shot through the window, through Logan's head. No time to suffer, died instantly."

"May we all get that opportunity," Rae mumbled. There was no time for her mumbo jumbo.

"No giving up, Rae." Brady squeezed her.

"We need more weapons," Kenan said like captain obvious. No duh!

Brady looked at Tobey. "You remember that shed? It's Weapons-R-Us."

"Let's go," Selma ordered.

BANG.

They covered their mouths in shock. Tobey, Brady, and Rae darted into the bathroom while Kenan and Selma hid in the closet. Someone had kicked the front door open. Heavy footsteps, like someone wore boots in the summer, inched up the steps in a slow fashion, taunting them.

Selma gripped the knife in her hand, ready to attack. It had to be the killer toying with them. It had to be.

The floorboards creaked, and the doors squeaked every time the killer opened one. The footsteps got louder, then stopped in front of the bedroom. Selma held onto Kenan's hand. Why didn't they hide in the bathroom too? Now, the killer would get them first, but she wouldn't go down without a fight.

She looked at Kenan. Hopefully, they were on the same page as pouncing on the killer. The outsider kicked the door in, and Selma transformed into Xena the Warrior Princess. She yelled as she stabbed him in the heart. He managed to fire off a shot, barely missing her. A bullet hole decorated the wall.

Selma sat on top of the killer's thighs and repeatedly jabbed the knife in and out of his chest. Blood spurt everywhere. "Die! Die! Die!" All she spotted was red from blood, from rage. She sought revenge for making her weekend hell.

Kenan knelt down to the floor on the other side of the dead body; he looked in despair. "Selma, stop."

"He killed our friends, and tried to kill us!"

"Selma, stop!" Kenan raised his voice. "He's the fucking ranger. He could've helped us!"

Out of her black-out, Selma noticed the light green uniform. She covered her mouth. Oh no. She'd get jail time for this. Why hadn't he introduced himself?

Wait, he probably drove. In urgency and panic, Selma searched the guy's pockets and found the keys. She ditched the knife in his chest, opting to take the gun as she sprinted down the stairs.

Kenan chased after her. "Selma!"

She hopped in the driver's seat while he opened the passenger's side door. "I'll radio for help."

"No time. We have to get outta here!"

Kenan folded his arms across his chest. "I'm not leaving Rae."

"Then get out of my way!" Selma started the car engine.

He jumped in. He reached for the steering wheel to prevent her from leaving. "It'll take me a second to get everyone."

"No fucking time!" It wasn't Selma's problem that they didn't rush out the other room when they heard all the commotion. She put the car in drive and sped off without waiting for Kenan to close the door.

He touched the wheel again.

"Try that again, and I swear I'll shoot you!"

He glared at Selma with fiery eyes. "What's your fucking problem?"

Not enough time to answer that question. Selma turned on the high beams, so she could see the path clearer. She was used to driving on paved roads, not beat down, dirt trails. Too many curves and deep dips caused the car to rock back and forth. She was getting carsick; it'd probably help if she'd slow down, but Selma's foot refused to ease off the pedal.

The ranger wasn't the killer, so there was still some sick bastard out there with a bow and arrow. Or worse yet—a sniper gun. This moving vehicle was probably his target. She had to get the hell out of dodge.

Rae, Tobey, Kenan, and Brady would just have to understand, she reasoned.

Selma kept her eye on Kenan, at least his shadow, through her peripheral vision in case he tried something funny.

He snatched the microphone from the center of the console. "Hello, hello. We need help. A killer is stalking me and my friends. Hello." They waited for a response. When none came, he threw the device at the window. "Damn it!"

Mr. Calm, Cool, and Collected seemed on the verge of a mental breakdown. "Don't break it; we need it."

"Says the person who killed the fucking ranger!" Kenan punched the dashboard. "Selma, pull over! Stop the car!"

Out of defiance, she pressed harder on the pedal. She went too fast during a curve, almost rolling the car over.

"Stop the car! We need to go back for Rae!"

Forget Rae, she'd have to take care of herself. If she had stolen the car, would Kenan pressure her to go back for Selma? Hell no.

They drove a good distance—probably twenty miles or so—before Kenan lost his patience. Instead of verbally pleading for Selma to turn around, he decided to go after what he wanted. Grabbing the wheel and forcing a sharp turn took Selma by surprise. They veered and crashed into a gigantic tree; the air bag knocked Selma unconscious.

"THEY LEFT US! THEY left us!" Rae looked around the room in bewilderment. She knew they were in trouble, stranded once more. The ranger dead. Maybe she had been right all this time—Selma was the killer. Otherwise, why would she eliminate the only person who could help them?

Selma had a partner, maybe missing Adam. It was no coincidence that he disappeared, unless an outsider, like RL, really did capture him.

Never in a million years would she think Kenan would desert her, even if to get help. Not only did he abandon her, but also he ditched his best friend, Tobey. He chose love over family; Rae frowned.

She shook her head. No more being wimpy. No more woe is me crap. Rae's friends needed her assistance to flee these damn woods. She'd fight to protect them. She should've executed what she set out to do earlier in the day. She probably would've been to a neighbor's home by now. She could have traveled in the day instead of nighttime. "Does anyone have a flashlight?"

"Why?" Tobey rubbed the back of his neck, glancing out the window.

"We have to walk outta here."

Brady grabbed Rae's hand. "Do you think that's a good idea with a lunatic carrying a bow and arrow out there somewhere? The light will make us easy targets."

"Well, we're sitting ducks if we wait here. You were right, Brady, no giving up." Rae held hands with Brady and Tobey. "We have to try for Naomi, Logan, and Marissa. They need a proper burial. To make sure that happens, we can't be laying down next to them." Her frustration and anger over being left fueled her determination to make it out alive.

The guys shared a look.

"The flashlight?" Rae repeated.

"I think it's downstairs," Tobey answered.

"Good. We need to put on layers of clothes to keep from freezing. Wear sneakers if you have any, and whoever makes it downstairs first, grab bottles of water."

"We need weapons," Brady said.

Tobey released his friend's hand, bent down, and yanked the bloody knife out of the ranger's chest. "Here's something."

"And there's weapons in the shed," Brady added.

"Then we'll have to make our way over there first. It's closer if we try a neighbor, but if no one's home, we're out of luck." Rae gulped. Her decision could make or break the escape plan.

Was it wise to try neighbors she hadn't seen in years? Would they even be the same people? What if the locals were torturing her friends, and she'd walk them right into a trap? Maybe instead of going the shorter, easier route, she should suck it up and go the distance to ensure getting out the woods completely. Then they'd be at a highway.

Rae wanted to hide the doubt in her facial expression but didn't know if she succeeded. To get more time to think in private, she urged the guys to be productive and complete the tasks she asked of them earlier.

Brady touched her cheek. "I'm not leaving you alone."

"We'll finish faster if we split up," Rae said.

"Brady's right. We can't leave each other; Kenan would never forgive us if anything happened to you," Tobey said.

Tears formed in her eyes; she avoided their gazes. If that were true, she would be sitting in that car, counting down the minutes before seeing a police or park ranger station.

They took turns adding layers of clothing in each bedroom. During Tobey's turn, they made her wait in the hallway. Brady was the only one who didn't have sneakers. Rae felt bad for him because he'd have blisters the size of Montana. She kicked the side of the bed; there was no way he could make a thirty-mile hike.

"Wait. Logan wore New Balance. I don't know if you two are the same size, but it'll have to do." Tobey was a genius.

Rae, Tobey, and Brady cautiously made their way into the living room, crawling on all fours, knowing full well the killer could be waiting to strike again. The door off the hinges didn't help any.

Brady leaned over Logan's body, held his nose, then sat on the floor. He turned away from the corpse and gagged. "I can't...I can't touch him."

Poor Logan. He had expressed his feelings to Rae. Now, he was gone, never to remember any of it. She eyed his body like someone witnessing a horrific accident. So many things she wished she could've said to him. She prayed for her friends; hopefully, they were in Heaven and not stuck in Purgatory. Would this be the last time Rae would ever see them? Could the rest of the group make it out alive, or was it just a hopeless dream?

Tobey inched over to Logan's legs and pulled socks and sneakers off his feet. He handed them to Brady, who gagged again, while taking them.

Hesitantly, he put the belongings on his feet. "Sorry, Logan," he whispered.

Rae felt a lump in her throat, glancing over at the empty couch. She had to hold it together. "Water, then we can go."

The guys nodded. They followed her into the kitchen. She grabbed all the water bottles out of the refrigerator and put them in her empty book bag. Tobey took it, so she wouldn't have to carry anything heavy.

"Wait, the flashlights." Brady crawled back into the living room then returned. Rae and Tobey were already by the back exit. Brady held a flashlight and handed the other one to Rae. She reached for the doorknob.

"Wait." Tobey lowered her hand. He took a deep breath, then peeked his head out the glass pane. Scanning outside, he must not have seen anything suspicious because he said, "Coast's clear" after opening the door.

He left first, then Rae, last was Brady, who closed the door behind him. The full moon and stars illuminated white light in the yard. Beyond the trees, total darkness.

Rae looked at the blanket still in the same spot. Brady tapped her arm as if pleading for her to lead the way. She stepped low in front of Tobey and crept to the Jeeps.

They'd need another weapon, and she knew exactly where to find one. She maneuvered behind the Jeeps. Tobey and Brady shadowed her moves; they formed a single line like kids in elementary school. Rae crawled on her knees. She made her way to the bushes and pulled the knife out of its hiding place. "Found it."

"Found what?" Brady whispered.

"A knife."

"How did you know it'd be here?" Tobey asked.

"Earlier today, Selma and I found it. A long story that I can share on our hike outta here." She curled her fingers, urging them to follow her. They could stop walking low to the ground once trees could hide them a little. Once they weren't out in the open.

Rae would have never imagined the dark shadows would scare her, but there she was terrified, pretending to put on a brave face. Tree branches looked like skeletal, pointy fingers willing to snatch them. She listened closely for leaves crackling or tree limbs snapping, anything to indicate someone or an animal may be following or approaching them.

Eventually, they reached the shed. She remembered this place; it was her family's. She scanned the room; the flashlight revealed sharp objects hanging. Whoa, who stocked it with all this stuff? Brady wasn't lying when he had said it was full of weapons.

Tobey shut the door. "Each grab something, then let's go. Right, Rae?"

"We should stay."

"What?" Tobey asked as him and Brady turned to face her simultaneously.

"Just for a little while to rest." She breathed heavily. "You have no idea how daunting this hike will be."

Brady nodded. "I'm hungry. Damn, why didn't we think to grab something to eat?"

A sly grin formed on Tobey's lips. "I don't know about you guys, but I brought snacks." He dug candy bars, protein bars, and small bag of chips from his hoodie pocket. "There's more where this came from, so dig in." He handed each of them something, and they devoured their snacks as if they had no home training.

"We need to sit and rest our legs just for a little bit. Try to sit on the floor away from the windows." Rae gulped once she realized there were no blinds. All the killer had to do was approach the shed and they'd be visible, but they had to take the chance. She switched off their only light source just in case. Brady winced before he joined Rae on the floor. He patted her knee, so she returned the gesture. Tobey was across from them; he played with his knife.

"I'm sorry about Naomi," she whispered.

Tobey wiped a tear. "She was my life. Whoever killed her will get what's coming to him. I'll have no mercy on Adam." Rae and Brady looked in each other's direction. "I suppose it was him. He got loose, right?"

"I'm sorry, Tobey, but...I don't think it's ever been Adam." Tears formed in Rae's eyes. "I think it's an outsider, a local, or neighbor. I mean, how could Adam have gotten a bow and arrow? Sure, he could hide a knife in his bag, but a bow. No way...that's why we should get some rest. I mean, we shouldn't attempt to go to a neighbor's cabin anymore. We should make our way out of the woods entirely."

"Maybe someone will come looking for that ranger. Maybe we should stay put," Brady said.

"No, we have to escape like Kenan and Selma did," Rae said.

"I trust you, Rae. Do you trust me and Brady?" Tobey held his breath, waiting for an answer.

"Of course."

"Then tell us how you knew where to find a knife."

She lowered her gaze to the weapon. She explained how earlier she and Selma fought, then came upon the knife and shredded pieces of the Jeeps' belts.

"And you're just telling us now?" Brady asked in a panic.

"I'm sorry." Rae pouted. "It was our way of trying to narrow down the killer."

Tobey crossed his arms over his chest. "And how did that go for you?"

If she wasn't careful, she may have a mutiny on her hands. "I'm sorry. I wish I would've done things differently."

Brady caressed her hand. 'We all do."

"You two should take a power nap while I'll be watchman. Maybe we each take twenty-minute intervals? That gives us enough time to take it easy and see if someone comes looking for the ranger. How does that sound?" Tobey proposed.

"How can I sleep in here?" Brady asked in disgust.

"Trust me, Brady, just close your eyes. You'll wish you had once we start our journey. I'm talking at least three days. I mean the whole nine yards." Rae squeezed his hand.

She had to put her trust in Tobey since her eyelids felt heavy. She was sore. If she got some shuteye, the pain would go away temporarily.

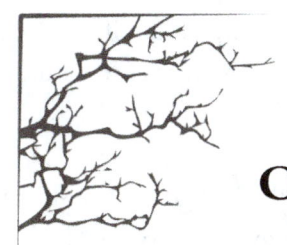

# Chapter Twenty-Eight

Adam finished inspecting the entire cabin. He had came across Naomi and a stranger—must have been when he heard the gunshot—upstairs, while Logan, at least he thought that was him; his face was partly removed, lay downstairs. Bloody footprints painted the floorboards. All this happened while he hid in the closet? Would he have died if he hadn't gotten loose?

Adam recalled overhearing people say they should get layers of clothing, so he ran back upstairs for extra clothes. He wasn't staying in haunted central. Probably nothing but vengeful ghosts. At least in their last moments Marissa, Naomi, and Logan realized Adam wasn't really the killer.

He bounced up and down to hype himself up. Grow a set. Be a man. He'd have to enter the woods alone in the complete dark, at least until he bumped into someone else. He'd have to take his chances with the group, well, of who was left.

Adam strolled into the hallway; he stopped in front of Naomi and Tobey's old room. He cringed at the sight of her corpse. How did he not hear anything? He had been next door. Adam tried to come up with any clue—a cough, a sneeze, a voice—but he couldn't wrap his brain around anything. The killer was a silent one, even more scary and creepy.

He'd probably regret it, but he needed to get a closer look. Lowering his eyes to the stained floor, Adam spotted something silver under the bed. As if calling his name and putting him in a trance, he entered the room, bent down, and retrieved the mysterious object.

A tape recorder? Finally a clue unless Naomi and Tobey were one of those kinky couples, who recorded and videotaped their sexual fantasies. He rewound a little bit then pressed play. A guy crying. The same sound from earlier.

Did he record himself, or was he never there in the first place? The clever fucker. Silent killer indeed. Adam could be a jerk, and not warn anyone about this new evidence. He could say "fuck you" for accusing him. However, if he wanted to survive, then he needed other people. Couldn't help Adam if they're all dead, and they wouldn't stop dying if they didn't wise up. This clue would finally help them do that.

If only he could get to them in time, Adam thought.

He sprinted downstairs and out the door. He knew how to get to the shed and lake; if they weren't in one of those areas, then they were all out of luck. Adam ran like an Olympian track star. His eyes adjusted to the darkness. Maybe it'd be best to sneak up on them. He slowed down to a speed walk. Almost to the shed, he could hardly breathe, panting while crouching down with his hands on his knees.

But he couldn't afford to take a break. Seconds couldn't be wasted. He crept on his tiptoes toward the shed. What was he getting himself into? Adam approached the window and peered inside. Tobey, who stared at Brady and Rae, held a knife in his hand. They seemed to be sleeping, unless they were already dead, and he was admiring his work.

Tobey turned his head. They made eye contact. Adam could tell that Tobey's eyes were full of evil and hatred.

In fear, Adam backed away from the window and ran. So much for being a hero, he scolded himself.

*Crackle. Crackle. Snap. Snap.*

He suspected Tobey wasn't far behind. Why didn't he grab a weapon earlier?

Tobey jerked Adam backwards by his hoodie, gagging him like yesterday. Adam choked and reached out for his throat to loosen the grip. Tobey spun him around. "Why are you running?"

"Why are you chasing me?" Adam moaned, trying to measure Tobey's strength. If he could strike his opponent where it'd count the most, then maybe Tobey would drip the knife. Wide-eyed, he gasped for air.

"Because you're a fucking killer, and everyone else may be on board about letting you go, but I'm not a supporter of that."

Adam gulped. "Tobey, I didn't kill her. I promise you." He raised his hands in surrender.

"There you go again with 'her.' Say Naomi's name."

"Naomi! I'm sorry. Please don't kill me!"

Tobey shook Adam. "Keep your voice down."

"Sorry," he mumbled.

Tobey grinned. "It's funny that you're begging for your life when you're the fucking killer."

"I didn't kill anyone and deep down you know that." Adam raised the tape recorder in the air.

Tobey snatched it, laughing like a hyena. He cracked his neck. "You're right. No more pretending. It wasn't supposed to be this way, you know. No one else was supposed to come. Only friends." He stared off into the distance with a blank stare. "I tried to get you to leave, but you're a dumb fuck. Why you stayed is beyond me. A fatal mistake."

Fatal. Oh, shit. "You were gonna let me leave. Well let me. I promise I won't tell anyone. Please let me go. Follow through with the plan."

"It's too late."

"It's never too late," Adam pleaded, a tear slid down his cheek.

"Tell everyone I said 'hi.' I'll be seeing you guys soon." Tobey stabbed him in the chest multiple times then slit his throat. Adam threw up blood. He gasped for his last, final breath.

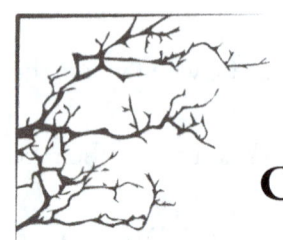

# Chapter Twenty-Nine

Brady woke up with no idea what time it was. He looked up at the window. Still darkness. Thankfully, no one was peeking in. He glanced at Rae, who rested on his shoulder. He could treasure this moment forever.

Where was Tobey? He was absent from the dingy shed. Brady decided to check things out. Maybe Tobey heard something? Maybe the killer got him? How could Brady protect him? He gazed down at his axe and machete. One of these would have to do. He moved slowly and placed Rae's head near the wall to not disrupt her sleep.

Brady took a deep breath, calling himself an idiot for going into a possible line of fire. He manned up and walked outside. Tobey stood with his back from the shed. His white hoodie looked like a gigantic marshmallow floating in thin air. Brady snuck up on him. "What kind of watchman are you?" Brady asked while Tobey hurriedly placed something into his hoodie pocket. "How you gonna keep an eye out on things if you're facing the opposite direction?"

Brady stood in front of Tobey, so his eyes could stay on the shed.

Tobey sniffed. "I'm sorry. I thought I heard something, but it was nothing. And I can't stop thinking about Omi. She's gone. The love of my life is gone..."

He patted Tobey's hand, not knowing what to say. He couldn't be a heartless douche bag and tell Tobey to stop grieving, to stay focused so he could protect him and Rae. Between Rae and Tobey, Brady would have to be the strong one. Yeah right, he was scared shitless.

Tobey looked off to the side. "I was thinking you two should stay here. I'll go for help. That way if the police come, you won't miss them."

Brady shook his head. "We should stick together."

"Not when there's a faster chance for us to get help. Stay with Rae and keep her protected. I'll keep going straight—will end up somewhere eventually. Please let me do this...I have nothing to lose, nothing to live for, so if something happens to me, you guys will be safe."

Tobey had nothing to live for? That was the grief talking, exactly why he shouldn't go alone. He had no fight left. He could die or give up, and they would never know. It wasn't a good idea by any means.

Kenan and Selma escaped; they arrived at the police station by now. The cops were probably on their way right this second. No point getting exhausted trying to walk out of here when they could just wait it out a little bit longer.

"So what do you think, dude? Will you make sure Rae stays safe?" Tobey asked.

Brady shook his head.

"Come on, dude. I'm telling you what I'm doing. It's not like I'm asking. It's not like you can stop me. I'm leaving now." Tobey patted Brady on his shoulder. "It'll give you enough time to come up with a story for Rae before she wakes up. I can trust you, right?"

Brady nodded. It's not as if he could tie Tobey up; his friends used that tactic on Adam, and look how that worked out.

He raised his eyebrow. What didn't Tobey want him to see in his pocket? "Need anything?" He fished for information on the sly.

Tobey lifted his weapon in the air. "No, I think I got everything." He laughed. "Not everyone can be fully loaded like you."

"It's not funny; I'm protecting myself."

"And that's a good thing, but you better protect Rae. If something happens to her, then Kenan will kill you."

In a defensive tone, Brady said, "Then he shouldn't have left her."

"I'm sure that wasn't a part of the plan. He had his reasons."

"Is that a phone?"

"What?"

Brady pointed to Tobey's pocket. "Is that a phone?"

"Uh...yeah. When I'm out far enough, I'll be able to call for help." Tobey wiped sweat from his forehead. "Speaking of that, I should head out." He left in a hurry. Brady sighed, praying his friend would have good luck.

KENAN WATCHED SELMA sleep. He fiddled with the gun in his hands. She's lucky it didn't go off during their impact, he thought.

Why did Selma have to be stupid and split the group up?

He couldn't bring himself to leave her alone, even if she wasn't aware of her surroundings at the moment. He'd wait patiently for her to wake up, hoping Tobey and Brady had his sister's back. He removed his hoodie and placed it over her cold body. Wearing a short sleeve shirt, Kenan shivered. His stomach growled.

Kenan stopped staring at Selma long enough to look straight ahead into total blackness, then glanced up at the moon. He had no idea where they were, no visible landmarks, and neither brought a flashlight. If she woke up tonight, they'd have to navigate in the dark just like when he had to venture off alone the first night to grab Marissa and Brady.

A slight smile formed on his lips. He had gotten closure from his ex, and it felt so good. Back to reality, Kenan grimaced. Mar was dead. He imagined her ghost appearing in front of the car, not in color, in black and white, possibly gray.

Kenan could barely keep his eyes open. He blinked rapidly, hoping that spark of energy would help, but it didn't. He closed his eyes, only to rest for a few seconds. Only a few seconds, he promised himself.

THE SUNRAYS BEAMING down on Kenan awakened him. It felt like he was stranded on Mars. He glanced over at Selma, who rubbed her forehead as if she was in excruciating pain. Bruises and dried blood covered her face, giving the illusion of chicken pox.

"Good morning," Kenan said.

She rose in her seat; his hoodie fell to her lap. "Did we sleep here all night?"

"It looks like it."

She reached for the microphone. "We need to call for help."

Kenan snatched it away. "It doesn't work, remember? We have to go back for them. I hope you know that."

"I'm not going back there." Selma folded her arms across her bloodstained tank top. "It's not safe, Kenan. We're so close; we have to keep moving."

"Not without Rae, Tobey, and Brady."

"They're probably dead by now."

Kenan dropped the gun on his lap and grabbed both of her shoulders. He shook her. "Take it back!"

"Get off of me!" Her eyes widened, and she flinched.

"Take it back! You better pray Rae isn't hurt!"

"I'm sorry. I didn't mean it."

Kenan took a deep breath and cracked his neck. He looked relieved, releasing Selma. He picked the firearm back up. "I have the gun now, so it looks like I'm calling the shots, but unlike you, I'll actually give the other person a choice. I'm going to find them. You can stay here and wait or try to make it out of the woods alone."

"Kenan—"

"What's your decision?"

She rubbed his arm. "I know you don't want to hear anything I say because I left Rae, but please think logically instead of emotionally. Going back would be suicide."

Kenan touched the side of Selma's face gently then gave her a tender kiss. "Goodbye, Selma." He opened the car door and walked away.

Selma opened the door. She chased after him, pleading, "Please don't leave me alone."

He turned around. "Come with me, then you won't be alone."

She cried, a truly vulnerable moment. She unraveled right before his eyes, no longer the feisty badass she claimed to be. "I can't. I don't want to die." Selma lowered her eyes to the ground. "The way you'll do anything to protect Rae, is the same way I feel about seeing my mom again. Please, Kenan. We're the only family we have left. I can't leave her."

"I understand...if you keep straight, you'll be out of here in no time." Kenan wiped a tear. "Pace yourself; there's probably like ten miles left."

"Kenan, please," Selma whispered.

"Keep straight and you should be fine."

"At least give me the gun."

Kenan looked down at the weapon in his hands. "I can't do that, Sel. I need it for protection. You're heading to safety while I have to backtrack towards the danger zone; all because you left people behind."

Selma frowned. "I said sorry."

"And hopefully one day you'll actually forgive yourself." He gave a weak smile then left.

*Crackle. Crackle. Snap. Snap.*

Kenan's grin grew wider—maybe he'd get closure as he did with Mar.

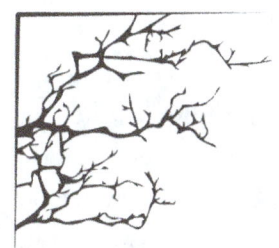

# Chapter Thirty

Selma dreaded every second hiking back into the 'danger zone.' If only she had a weapon. She and Kenan had slept the night away. Who knew if the killer found them? He probably waited at the end of the woods, so close to freedom, ready to kill them with a knife or bow and arrow. Selma wasn't stupid. This maniac was a smart psychopath. He loved toying with them.

If only they hadn't had that lovers' spat that led to her kicking Kenan to the curb. If that nightmare never happened, then she could have used her womanly charms to get her way. Kenan loved Selma; there was no way he'd fall out of love easily, right?

Maybe it wasn't too late. They were probably only a mile or two away from the car. Women won when guys were swayed by their small brain, a.k.a. penis.

A squirrel ran past her feet. She licked her lips. Mashed potatoes with gravy teased her taste buds. Her mouth felt dry, and she held her stomach when it roared.

"I admire you and your mom's close bond. I often wonder how different my life would've been if I hadn't lost my mom," Kenan whispered. When Selma didn't respond, he stared at her then playfully bumped into her shoulder. "I'll get you out of here. I promise."

Selma nodded, wiping a tear away. This was the sweet, romantic guy she fell in love with. The guy who put other people's needs first. She wrapped her arm into his. "I'm sorry for everything."

"Me too." He touched her arm and squeezed it.

They both remained silent until Kenan broke the ice. "I'm surprised Rae took everyone's deaths so well. I thought she'd try to end her life just to join them. That's why I had such a tight grip on her this weekend. I couldn't afford to lose her yet."

Yet?

"She's stronger than you think."

Kenan smiled. "She's very unpredictable, but not a killer."

"I know. There's no way she was capable of this," Selma agreed even though in the back of her mind she figured Rae could have pulled it off with the help of Adam or RL. She couldn't afford to say that though and have a repeat of the bathroom fight. Selma frowned and stepped to the side, creating distance between them.

He snatched her by the arm, pulling her closer. "No stay close, Sel...I admire that you're strong and have a mind of your own. There was never a dull moment in dating you."

"Was?"

"Yeah past tense. You dumped me, remember?" he said matter-of-factly like a robot. No hint of disdain or sadness.

"People say things they don't mean out of anger."

"So we're not broken up?"

"Not if you don't want to be," she reasoned. She'd say or do anything to stay on the good side of the person with the weapon.

"If only it was that simple to go back to how things were." He shook his head.

"Why can't it?"

"I can't forget that you didn't trust me or Rae this weekend. You even tried to turn everyone against us. Spit in my face...I love you, Selma, but I can't look at you the same way. You're not ride or die like I thought."

Selma frowned. "You can't forgive me, but you can forgive Marissa. She cheated on you."

Kenan stopped abruptly. "Did you hear that?" He scanned the area.

She strained her hearing. In the near distance, leaves crunched under someone's foot, also a low whistle escaped someone's lips. She widened her eyes, moved closer to Kenan, and squeezed his waist. "It's the killer."

Kenan guided them to a tree to stand behind. Selma leaned her back against it while he stood in front of her. He held the gun and steadied his feet in case he needed to use it. Selma quivered with nerves. They weren't going to make it!

They anticipated the killer coming from the right side of the woods, so they both stared intensely in that direction. She covered her mouth, so she wouldn't make a noise and blow their cover.

To Selma's surprise, Tobey, with a pep in his step, sauntered past the tree as if he was carefree. He held a knife loosely to the side, blood all over it. She flinched, probably the same one that slain Naomi and the ranger. Selma burned so many bridges that no one would have her back now. They'd all rat her out, and she'd have to spend her prison sentence in some small town.

Kenan did a double take, flabbergasted. He caught her gaze. He followed Tobey. She took off after her boyfriend. They tiptoed for a minute or two.

Kenan said, "Hey, Tobey, you're an easy target, not even realizing people are sneaking up on you." Tobey turned around, and the boys shared a pat on the back.

Tobey hugged Selma and planted a kiss on her cheek.

"Where's everyone?" Kenan asked in a somber tone.

Tobey lowered his eyes to the ground. "I'm sorry, man. We thought you guys got of here to get help. I told them to wait at the shed while I got help too, at least out far enough to get cell phone reception."

"Rae's at the shed?"

"Yeah."

"How can you be so sure?"

Tobey gulped. "I told them to stay put."

Kenan slapped his forehead. "Geez Louise, we're talking about my sister here. She's probably convinced Brady to leave; you know he can't say 'no' to her."

"She didn't think it'd be safe to try a neighbor, so she wanted to walk outta here. They could very well be on their way." Tobey looked at Selma. "Why aren't you guys safe somewhere?"

"We crashed a couple miles back. Speedy Gonzalez wouldn't turn around to get you guys."

"That's why you're backtracking?" Tobey asked as if contemplating a mystery.

Enough of the reunion, they had to get out of there. "Can we walk and talk at the same time?" Selma asked.

"I'm going back for Rae; you guys go ahead without me. Selma really wants to get out of here. Tobey, will you go with her? Protect her?"

Tobey nodded.

Kenan stepped closer to Selma and gave her a hug. "You misunderstood. I already forgave you a while ago. See you soon," he whispered in her ear.

She smiled then let go even though she didn't want to. Kenan was making a mistake going back. A deadly mistake.

He left. Selma and Tobey watched him disappear off into the distance. Tobey glanced at her. "Let's get out of here," he said.

She sighed in relief. "Please."

They headed in the opposite direction. A knife wasn't particularly better than a gun, but a knife was better than no weapon at all. Or was it?

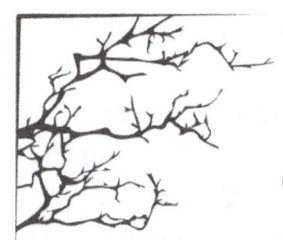

# Chapter Thirty-One

Rae loathed being told what to do. Of course, there was a difference between asking politely and ordering someone around. The latter was unreasonable in her mind; that's why the second Brady revealed that Tobey demanded they stay at the shed, she said," Hell no." They needed to search for him. He shouldn't be by himself. Plus, they were stronger in numbers. She grabbed a hammer while Brady insisted on keeping his two weapons.

All night, Brady had stayed at the same pace as Rae with hardly any complaints. She was worried about him because constant complaining was his MO. He seemed like a pod person.

"Do you need a water break?" she asked.

"Nah, I'm good. The sooner we get of here, the better."

"Hate to break it to you, but we still have a ways to go."

Brady panted, wiping sweat from his forehead. "A water break sounds good then."

Rae smiled and locked arms with him, leading him to a huge tree stump. He leaned up against it and slid down to bend his knees. Rae pulled a bottle out of her backpack and handed it to him. Brady splashed water on his face, moaned in ecstasy, then gulped down his drink. "That felt so good." He closed his eyes to enjoy the moment. He opened them, looking at Rae. "I'm sorry I'm slowing you down."

She slid down to be eye level with him. "Thanks for not leaving me."

He touched her cheek. "Never."

Rae closed her eyes and knew he was speaking the truth. The wind vibrated the tree under them like a bumpy car ride; they gazed at each other.

The Orgasm Tree. Brady got to visit after all.

"You sly girl. I knew you wanted to take me here." Brady gave a wide grin. "Can you imagine making love and feeling this at the same time? Talk about a double whammy."

Rae blushed. He thought she planned this, which wasn't the case at all. She was surprised just like him.

"Kenan was right; the Orgasm Tree is awesome." He closed his eyes.

She didn't want to burst his happy bubble, but she needed to know the truth. "Speaking of orgasm, did you and Mar have sex the night she died?"

Brady sighed, splashing water on his face again. "Adam told you that, didn't he? He just wanted to turn everyone against me."

"So it's not true?"

Brady bit his bottom lip. He avoided eye contact with Rae. "I don't want to lie to you."

She stood up and glared down at him. "Oh my God, you did. You did sleep with her. Adam wasn't lying."

Rae ran as fast as she could while Brady chased her. "Rae, wait! Please wait! Let me explain!"

The one person she could trust, besides her brother, was a liar. A convincing liar—who knew what else Brady faked? He was waiting for her to put her guard down, then he would strike. She shouldn't have fallen for his charms.

The trees and shrubbery were a blur as she sprinted past, making sure to zigzag, so he couldn't follow closely behind. Sooner or later, Brady would tire out, especially since he kept yelling. *That's right buddy—use all your energy.*

"Rae, please! Rae!"

She moved faster; it was a matter of life or death. She ignored her back pains caused by the backpack slamming into it. Unfortunately, Brady didn't show any signs of slowing down soon. She felt dehydrated; she should have drunk water and ate a protein bar when she had the chance. Rae hid behind a tree, holding her hammer in an upright position, in case she needed to strike Brady. Tears strolled down her cheeks. What if Tobey didn't flee on his own? What if Brady murdered him while she was asleep? That's why there was no trace of him. If Rae wasn't alert, she wouldn't make it either.

Brady's footsteps calmed down. He was walking instead of running. He was too smart to fall for her trick. It'd be better to emerge so she could see his whereabouts, instead of him sneaking up on her. Rae treaded to the side, away from her hiding place. He dashed towards her.

"Stop!"

He paused. "Rae, let me explain. I'd never hurt you."

Only her close friends.

Rae aimed her hammer at him. "Prove it."

"What?"

"Prove it. Drop your weapons and step aside."

Brady released the axe and machete then stepped forward. He didn't even glance down at them. Rae circled him and kicked the weapons behind her. He put his hands up in surrender. "Can I talk now?"

"You got five seconds before I bash your face in."

"It's like that. Really, Rae? It's me. It's Brady. I don't have a violent bone in my body." He placed his hands in his pockets, shaking his head.

"But you're a liar."

"I had to lie about hooking up with Marissa. You didn't see everyone's paranoia. They were gonna kill Adam until Kenan stopped them. If they believed Adam, then I'd be next. I lied to protect myself. You, of all people, should understand that. I lied to them, but I can't lie to you. I trust you even though you don't trust me." Brady gulped. "Put the hammer down, please."

Rae ignored his request.

"Damn it, Rae. Really? When I left the lake, she was alive. Kenan was left alone with her, then Adam. Why would I kill Marissa? Or anyone for that matter?" Brady smirked and wiped a tear from his eye. "If I'm gonna die, I'd rather it be by your hands. At least I hope you'll make it quick and won't torture me."

"That's not funny. This is no time for jokes." She frowned.

"Well, what am I supposed to do?" He scratched his head. "You went all Selma on my ass. It hurts that you, of all people, think I'm capable of murder."

"Walk in my shoes for a minute. You tell me that Tobey left to get help, but there's been no sign of him. He couldn't have gotten that much of a head start on us."

"He did leave, Rae, and he said I couldn't stop him. What did you want me to do, tackle him?"

She cocked her head to the side like a chicken, then grabbed Brady by the collar of his shirt. She pushed him backwards toward a tree. She put her finger to her mouth, signaling him to be quiet. She could hear footsteps, and since he was wide-eyed, he could hear someone approaching too.

The person was on the other side of the woods. It was as if someone, possibly the killer, was jogging or something. "We have to keep moving. If we follow that path, it'll lead us to higher ground, then we can probably find Tobey faster. If the killer hasn't gotten to him first," Rae whispered.

Brady looked hopeful. "So you believe me now?"

She had no choice but to trust him. Brady was all she had, and he sounded sincere when he had pleaded his case.

TOBEY AND SELMA MADE good leeway, walking at the same pace. They hiked the two miles to reach the car. There was a dented bumper and cracked windows. Both doors remained open. "How did the crash happen?" he asked.

"Kenan grabbed the wheel."

"Why?"

"He wanted me to turn around for Rae."

"If you would've waited for us, that never would've happened."

She rolled her eyes. "Not you too."

"The truth hurts, sweetie."

"Don't call me sweetie." Selma paced faster.

Tobey grinned. What a bitch. It'd be fun killing her. "Hey wait up. I have the knife, remember?" He caught up to her. "How does it feel to be wrong about this whole trip?"

She crossed her arms over her chest, making eye contact with him. If looks could kill. "I don't follow."

Tobey laughed. "You were wrong about the killer. How does it feel?"

"I apologized to Kenan already, but at least I made guesses. At least I was proactive in finding the killer."

"Like coming up with that idiotic plan with Rae to keep the hidden belts a secret."

Selma sighed, rolling her eyes again. "Of course, she told you. I knew she couldn't keep her mouth shut."

He smirked. "You know, if you weren't such a bitch, the other girls would've given you a chance."

Selma stopped in her tracks. "Excuse me?" She put her hands on her hips.

"You heard me; I didn't stutter. If you weren't such a *bitch* then Naomi, Marissa, and Rae would've given you a chance." Tobey walked away. He kicked a rock out of his way.

"Since we're giving tips, how about you hear this? If you weren't a boring asshole, you'd have more friends."

"Has anyone ever told you not to insult the person with a weapon?" Tobey pointed the knife at Selma in a mocking way.

"Don't talk to me."

"Fine with me." He smiled when she rushed to get away from him.

Boring? Not him. Tobey's quiet nature was a blessing. If he wasn't always thinking, then he couldn't be plotting. Then he couldn't rise to the occasion and devise a plan B, C, or D when plan A went down the drain. Extroverts didn't have the discipline such as he; that's why they couldn't get anything accomplished.

When Tobey was about ten years old, his favorite spot was near the train tracks in an open field. He would bribe cats to follow him, dropping bits of food on the ground. Sometimes he'd tie the animals on the train tracks; at other times, he'd wait for the perfect timing and push them in front of the train. Either way, they'd be flat like a pancake. One day his five-year old neighbor caught him. Tobey didn't have problems killing him to protect his secret. That was his first murder.

He had been pretty crafty getting people to let their guards down, then striking violently. He killed all the way up to his teenage years before getting caught. His damn older sister had witnessed him suffocating their mother with a pillow. Tobey would've killed their father too, but the bastard had left them when he was a baby. His sister had called 911 unbeknownst to him. As punishment, she was his last victim before the police knocked the front door down.

How did Tobey get away with all of that? By being quiet. By not bringing attention to himself in the boring neighborhood. He played the system and managed to get the judge to place him in a psych ward. Therapy sessions were a part of his treatment, but his hot therapist only wanted to jump his bones. Not that Tobey complained. By his request, she convinced the head honchos to allow him to spend quality time outside on the wraparound porch. There he would stare at the woods, plotting his next serial killing. He was patient and could wait.

Since Tobey was under the age of eighteen, his records were sealed. It was pretty easy to make a new life for himself in West Virginia. If only his old therapist could see him now. He couldn't wait for the world to know what happened here, to make a name for himself. At the age of twenty-eight, he was old enough so his name could be released. No more hiding from sealed records. He was ready to leave this world with a bang.

They strolled with silent tension for a while before Tobey decided it was time to push Selma's buttons again. "You're not a very trusting person, huh? Did something happen in your childhood?"

"I asked you not to talk to me."

"I just want to understand you before you leave."

Looking puzzled, she stared at Tobey. "Where am I going?"

He patted Selma's shoulders. "You'll know soon enough."

It wasn't in her nature to let things slide, so she followed that remark with, "You shouldn't talk like that, Tobey. It's not funny. It makes you sound like a murderer."

"If I am a killer, you're up shit creek." A wide grin formed on Tobey's lips. "Selma, come on. I'm just kidding; loosen up."

She squinted her eyes, full of rage. "Well, don't play like that."

"Have any idea what happened to Adam?"

"If he's smart, he escaped this hell hole."

Adam wished he would've escaped, but it wasn't in the cards for him. Kenan would probably pass him hung up on a tree near the lake. Who knew? Maybe Rae and Brady didn't stay put. Maybe they found Adam first.

"How long do you think we have left?" Tobey cracked his neck.

Selma sighed. "Maybe eight or nine miles. Can you hang?"

"I can definitely hang. Can you?"

"I guess we'll see." She frowned. "Tobey, I'm sorry about Naomi. I never got a chance to tell you that."

"Thanks, but I'm at peace with it."

"What?"

"I accepted that Omi is gone, probably helped that it felt good killing Adam."

Selma's green eyes widened. "Please stop playing."

"He got loose and killed my baby. I found him and got revenge."

Selma gulped.

"You understand, don't you? I couldn't let him get away with killing Omi and Marissa. Please don't judge me. I never judged you for killing the ranger. You thought he was the killer and wanted to get revenge too. It's just that I happened to get the right person."

She nodded, smiling weakly. "I understand."

Tobey could tell she was just saying what he wanted to hear. What a judgmental bitch.

For now, he would play along. "Thank you." They walked a few more steps; he studied Selma. She wobbled on her feet like they hurt. She tried to act as though she was comfortable, but he could tell it was all a ploy. She wasn't a good faker, as he was. Now, it was time to up the ante. He grabbed her by the arm. Selma slightly jumped then composed herself. "Watch your step. Kenan would never forgive me if something ever happened to you."

"I think you have me and Rae mistaken."

"Perhaps I do." She gave Tobey a stern look. "Just kidding. Take a chill pill."

Selma made an effort to wiggle her arm out of his grip, but he wouldn't let go, pretending he hadn't noticed. "How can I chill when someone's trying to kill us? You're acting worse than Brady."

"Brady's not that bad. You may want to rephrase that comment because a boring asshole like me took it as a compliment."

"You can't take to heart when I called you an asshole; you had just finished calling me a bitch. Of course, I'm gonna retaliate," Selma said. "Tobey, can you let go of me? I can walk on my own."

"Not yet. There's bumpy ground ahead." He stared at her, who avoided eye contact. He could see the wheels turning in her head. He beamed with triumph.

"How do you know what's ahead?" she whispered.

"I've been here before. Who do you think stocked the shed? I had to canvas the area to know all the nooks and crannies to successfully accomplish my task."

Selma gasped. "What task?"

"Killing you all."

"Stop playing, Tobey! This isn't funny!" She wiped a tear.

"Deep down, you know I'm not joking. That's why you're crying."

Vultures pecked at a dead deer in front of their path. Weeds sprouted against rotten tree stumps.

Selma slapped his hand away. "Let me go!" She jerked out of his grip. It'd be more fun to chase her. Deep down, she'd want o get caught because it was in her nature to fancy hearing answers.

She sprinted away; Tobey trailed her. It didn't take long for him to seize her from the back.

"You're sick!"

"I take that as a compliment too. Rephrase." He grinned. "You know, Kenan left me alone with Marissa, but he was scared the group would turn on me. He wanted to protect me, makes Kenan a great best friend."

"No." She crumpled in his arms.

"Yes, dear. It was easy killing Marissa, Omi, and Logan. Plus, Adam. I'm on a roll. Lesson learned: never trust the quiet ones or leave a person alone when people are dying. Duh! So once again, how does it feel to be wrong about everyone?" he asked.

"No, no, no." So disappointing. Tobey thought firecracker Selma would have more fight than that. What a wimp. "Somebody help me! Help me!"

Ah, there's the fight. Good times. Good times.

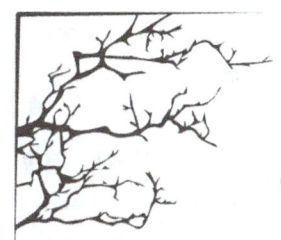

# Chapter Thirty-Two

"Did you hear that?" Brady asked. He and Rae hadn't spoken since the accusation, so he was happy to find any excuse to communicate with her again.

"What?"

Screams parroted in the distance.

Wide-eyed, Brady faced the direction the sound was coming from. "That."

"Be careful, Brady, animal traps are set out here. I think." She ran off and Brady followed. At first, she went a straight line then zigzagged close to the cliff's edge.

"Be careful, Rae."

"Shush!" She pointed down. "Tobey and Selma are down there." She grinned at Brady. "I told you we'd find him if we came up here."

"What is he doing?" Brady whispered. Things didn't look quite right down below. Why was Tobey holding Selma by the wrists while she tried to get away? He stepped backwards and ushered Rae to do the same. She was probably two seconds away from yelling their names. For some reason, that didn't seem like such a good idea. A pit formed in Brady's stomach.

Why was Selma there in the first place? Wasn't she and Kenan supposed to be long gone in the car, getting help by now? Brady frowned. What if Tobey and Selma were the killers? What if she killed Kenan? Rae would never be the same again.

But why murder everyone? It didn't make sense. Something shady was going on the way they argued. Brady looked at Rae and grabbed her arm. He wouldn't allow her to jump in case she got any bright ideas. She glanced at him for a split second, but he was too focused on the lower ground to enjoy the moment. Rae looked back down.

Tobey pushed Selma to the ground. She crawled away. He slit her Achilles heel—both of them. Rae covered her mouth, trying to make a run for it, but

Brady held her from behind. He was frozen in fear. However, he was smart enough to say, "Be still. He can't know we're here, or we're next."

"We have to help," she whispered.

"It's too late." By the time they would make it down the cliff, Selma would be long dead. If they made any noise to grab his attention, Tobey would still kill her. Then he'd be after them, and Brady was pretty self-aware to know he was too exhausted to run or fight back.

Selma's screeches would haunt Brady for the rest of his life. Tobey sliced her open like a pillowcase, waiting for feathers to fly out. Instead of feathers, it was blood, dark red blood. She had let out loud yelps before her final breath.

Not being able to digest anymore, Brady let go of Rae and regurgitated. He bent down, his body convulsed. Unfortunately, he gagged too loudly, so Tobey glanced up and saw them. Rae stood there hopeless while Brady continued to be sick.

Oh, shit. Once again, he let Rae down, he scolded himself.

Tobey rose to his feet, wiping the knife off with his shirt. "Hey, I thought I told you two to stay at the shed! It pays to listen!" He headed towards the trail that led to the top level.

Rae was wide-eyed; now, she was frozen in fear. "I told you we'd die, Brady."

"No, it's two against one; we can take him." He wiped his mouth. "Until then, run like hell!"

Instead of rushing straight to get out of the forest, she went towards the back of the woods. "Our only chance is to catch a neighbor!"

Without hesitation, Brady ran as fast as he could. He was never a track star though. He was medium built, looked good with a nice physique, but definitely not in shape. His laziness would come back to haunt him.

RAE AND BRADY HID INSIDE a mini-cave. They huddled, holding each other. They had to make quite a leap to reach the ground below, but it was worth the effort because it had thrown off Tobey. His footsteps quickened as he whistled above their heads.

Rae handed Brady a bottle of water. "Drink and rest your legs," she whispered.

He drank a sip. "I'm sorry—"

"Shush, he may still be near." She touched his knee. "There's nothing to apologize for. We're in this together."

He placed his head near hers; they shared a gaze.

Rae fought back tears. Kenan was gone; she couldn't imagine life without him. How could Tobey kill his best friend? That could be the only explanation why he wasn't around Selma and Tobey. Kenan's last few moments on earth were filled with betrayal.

For that, Tobey would have to pay.

If they wanted to kill Tobey, then they had to think smart. No more mistakes like bringing attention to themselves when they should've been hiding. What if that wasn't an accident? Or gag reflex? What if it was done on purpose? Rae could outsmart Tobey all day, everyday, but it wouldn't make a difference if he and Brady were working together.

Brady frowned. "Not again, Rae."

"What?" She bit her bottom lip.

"You're looking at me like you don't trust me. I'd never hurt you."

The last thing an obsessive psycho says before murdering his lover after she dumped him or disappointed him in some warped, twisted way. "You have to admit, it's sorta suspicious that you told me to be quiet, then you did everything in your power to get us noticed anyway."

His cheeks flushed red. "Sorry I couldn't hold it in. It's not like I'm used to watching people be tortured and brutally killed." Brady flinched. "Rae, please forgive me. I had a brain fart. Just know, I'll do everything in my power to protect you, and I'll spend the rest of my life apologizing until you forgive me, which isn't a long shelf life so please forgive me soon. Pretty please with sugar on top." He placed both hands together, pleading.

Damn his charms. It wasn't productive to stay mad for something he didn't mean. It wasn't Brady's fault that Rae was over-sensitive on matters like that. Plus, he could get one dig in. She had accused him of murder twice after all. She couldn't verbalize that she forgave him, but hopefully the smile was a great representative.

After figuring enough time had passed for it to be safe to leave their hiding place, Rae took the lead again. They both climbed up sharp boulders to reach higher ground. She had been right. Tobey was up ahead, searching for them. He turned his head side to side in a rapid motion.

As long as they stayed clear of the path and crept behind trees, then they'd stay hidden and could sneak up on him. Tobey stopped. Rae pulled Brady by the collar, pushing him up against a thick branch. She stood in front of him, holding her breath. Did Tobey sense he was being followed?

Even though she was curious about what he was doing, she wouldn't dare peek her head at Tobey. All they needed was for him to notice her. She stared into Brady's beautiful blue eyes and heightened her hearing. If Tobey stepped foot near her, she'd smash his head in.

If he stayed on the same path, Tobey was heading toward a neighbor's cabin; he probably assumed that's where Brady and Rae ran. That would have been the best decision, but Brady had ruined that.

THEY PURSUED TOBEY a good two miles without him realizing. Rae looked like a covert, sexy spy, maneuvering behind trees while Brady probably looked like a goofball. He was excited that the attacking-Tobey-from-behind scheme might actually work. He prayed to God that it would. Ironically, the birds on the ground didn't fly away, almost as though they didn't want to give away Rae and Brady's location. Like the birds wanted them to succeed as well.

Brady couldn't believe how strong Rae was being. He knew her brother was on her mind. She probably questioned when did Kenan pass away? Was it brutal like Selma's death? Did he fight back against his best friend? Brady felt sorrow for her; he wished he could tell Rae all those things, but he couldn't afford to have her lose concentration.

Rae stopped moving. "This is our chance to take him. I'll lure him out, then you get him from behind." She pointed to a path Brady should follow in order to successfully get behind Tobey without being seen.

Brady shook his head. "No, it's too dangerous."

"Any plan is too dangerous. We can only follow him for so long. If we do make it to another cabin, do you really think he's gonna let us go in and call the cops? It's now or never."

Damn it. She had more balls than he did. He promised himself he wouldn't let her down this time. He gulped. Life was too short. It was time to see if Rae could ever love him as much as he loved her. And no, not in a friendly way. It was now or never.

Brady stepped forward and kissed Rae passionately. To his surprise, she melted in his arms. This was the happiest moment of his life; he never thought sleeping in the Jeep could be topped, but he was wrong. He held her in his arms, and she touched her lips, smiling. "Good luck, Brady."

He grinned, winking. "Good luck to you too."

Before he could say anything else, Rae left her hiding place. He made his way to the dirt path to get in his position.

*Please work. Please work. Please work.*

Rae whistled, causing Tobey to spin around. "Rae, there you are. I've been looking for you all over," he said as if nothing ever happened. He began walking towards her.

Not backing down, she headed towards Tobey. "Been following you for a good two miles."

"Didn't hear you." Tobey shook his head. "How do you stay quiet in these damn woods?"

"Seriously, that's what you're asking me!" Rae slammed the hammer into the ground. "Why did you kill Selma?! Why did you kill my brother?!"

"You don't understand. You weren't supposed to see that."

She stuck out her middle finger. "Fuck you!"

"Where's Brady?"

"Calling the fucking police!"

"You're lying." Tobey smirked. "He wouldn't leave your side."

"Oh, really. We found the abandoned car and radioed for help. I told him to stay, so they could find him." She copied his smug facial expression. "I knew I could take you, you fucking wimp. Besides you know Brady does whatever I say."

Clapping, Tobey grinned. "Bravo! You're still not leaving this place, so you can wipe that smug look off your face."

"You're not making it out of here either."

He shrugged his shoulders. "Has it ever occurred to you that I don't want to?"

Huh? Rae was supposed to get the best of Tobey, distracting him, but he was confusing the hell out of both of them. He didn't want to leave? Well, his wish would come true soon. Maybe Tobey wouldn't fight back?

While tiptoeing slowly, Brady held his axe in position to strike. He held his breath, afraid any noise would tip Tobey off. He was so close that Brady could smell his body odor. Brady brought the axe down violently on his shoulder.

Tobey jerked back. "You fucking asshole!"

Brady raised the machete in his other hand; Tobey stabbed him in his upper arm and cut through his main artery.

"No!!!" Rae ran to both of them.

Brady stumbled back. Blood poured out like a waterfall. He was always an idiot and certainly not a hero, he scolded himself.

Rae smashed the hammer into Tobey's skull repeatedly. "Die! Die! Die!" She wouldn't stop even though his face was already bashed in, looked like road kill flattened by a car tire.

Brady didn't have enough energy to stop her; he lay on the ground. "Rae," he cried.

Out of her black-out, she crawled to kneel beside Brady. She held his hand and caressed his face. "Brady, I'm so sorry. I have to get help," she said in sorrow.

"Please don't leave me." He wasn't stupid. He'd be dead before help would arrive. If anyone had to be by his side for his last moment on earth, he was honored that it was Rae. Beautiful Rae, who would survive all this. That's all that mattered. "I love you, Rae."

She squeezed Brady's hand. "I love you too." She kissed his lips. Her tears fell on his face. Brady's heart beat quickened. *What triggered Tobey's killing spree?* His heart stopped.

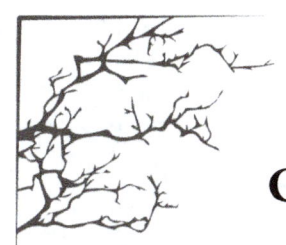

# Chapter Thirty-Three

It would have been logical to continue on the trail to a neighbor's house, but Rae didn't want to take a chance that no one was home. Now, she sat in the driver's seat of the ranger's car, crying into the dispatcher. How was she supposed to get out of here? The car wouldn't start, and she was too afraid to pop the hood to realize there was another missing part.

Rae held the button. "Please help me. My friends are all dead...my friends are all gone. It's only me." She released it; she tapped her foot, waiting for a response. "Please. Somebody. Anybody."

"Where's your location?" Static filled the other end. Rae explained her location, and the lady promised to bring help soon. She told Rae to stay put, not even asking what happened. How the others died. Nothing.

She probably assumed that Rae was the killer, who was turning herself in.

Rae held herself for comfort; her legs burned from all the hiking she did since last night. She was all alone. Tobey should've killed her and put her out of her misery.

Why did he do this? Now, she would never know.

She felt so weak that her head hung low. She smeared her hands with Brady's blood that painted her knees. If only they would've went to the beach instead.

The back of her head stung. Someone had hit her hard with something. Rae's eyes felt heavy. She fell out of the car, landing on her stomach, her vision too blurry to see who it was. Before she knew it, the person struck her again. She blacked out.

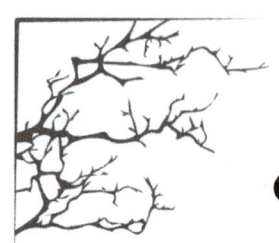

# Chapter Thirty-Four

Kenan sat on the dusty floor of the attic. He blocked the door. His sister, knocked out, lay on the other side of the room. The sunrays poured through the large window.

He watched Rae sleep peacefully and smiled to himself. People kept her safe just as they had promised. Rae returned to Kenan—all was right in the world again.

She opened her eyes and sluggishly positioned herself to sit upright. She rubbed the back of her head, her facial expression showed pain. She didn't have to worry any longer because soon there'd be no more suffering.

Rae blinked, wide-eyed. "Kenan!" She crawled over to him, and they hugged. "I thought you were dead. I'm so happy to see you."

"Why did you think I was dead?"

"Tobey—"

"Where is he?"

Rae lowered her eyes. She grabbed Kenan's hand and paused. "I killed him."

"Why?"

"Be—because he attacked Brady." Rae wiped tears from her eyes. The color red emerged on her face. "He killed our friends. I'm sorry, Kenan...Tobey was the killer."

Kenan stared at her.

"Did you hear me, Kenan?"

He nodded. "I heard you, but Tobey didn't kill everyone."

"I'm sorry, but I saw him murder Selma. She's dead."

"Was it brutal?"

"Yes."

Kenan grinned. "Good."

Rae looked shocked, backing away from her brother. "How could you say that?"

"She made your weekend miserable, so she had to pay. I asked Tobey to be rough with her." Kenan could tell the wheels were running in Rae's head. She was trying to take precaution but was never a poker player. "You're wrong. He didn't kill everyone. I admit I left Tobey alone with Mar—"

"But you blamed Adam?"

"I lied, Rae. I left Tobey alone with Mar, then I turned right back around. She was so happy and trusting. It wasn't difficult strangling her to death." He smiled. "Yes, Tobey watched, but he didn't participate. So get your facts straight, Tobey didn't kill everyone."

"How could you?" Rae stood up to leave, but Kenan gripped her arms and forced her away from the door. She wiggled out of his grasp and ran to the other side of the room.

Kenan sighed. "You have no room to be judgmental. You definitely didn't take it easy on Tobey, poor buddy."

"You were there?"

"You're not the only one who can trail behind someone without getting caught." He gave a smug smile. "I followed you and Brady from the Orgasm Tree." He frowned. "What's wrong, Rae? I orchestrated this all for you."

"No, Kenan! Don't you dare put me in this demented mess! You're fucking sick!"

"I'm your fucking brother. Show me some respect." He stomped over to Rae; he slapped her. "How can you not appreciate what I've done? I made sure our friends went to Heaven, so we won't be alone." He backed away from her. Crying, she held her arms. He blocked the door again. "You ungrateful bitch! Don't act like you don't know what today is!"

Ten years ago, this date to be exact, they had promised each other in this very attic in ten years if one of them wasn't living a happy life, then they both would end their lives to join their parents and not make the other one enter Heaven alone.

Kenan's stint in the psych ward in North Carolina made him obsessed with today. His therapist had said he needed to face the past to get closure. Well, today he'd finally get closure. Kenan's sister had never known he had been hospitalized. She always believed he stayed with their grandma. So naïve. He would tell Rae now, but she was acting out of line. How dare she not appreciate his sweet, brotherly gesture!

Tobey had lived down the hall from Kenan. He was fascinated that Kenan volunteered to stay in the psych ward instead of being forced. They became best friends after he revealed how his parents were murdered in their vacation home. Tobey would let him vent all day; he even had a sympathetic ear when Kenan cried about letting his sister down.

Per Tobey's request, the therapist convinced the head honchos that Kenan and Tobey were mentally stable to go out in society again. They were both twenty-five, just in time for Rae to head home from her four years away at college. It wasn't hard to convince Tobey to move to West Virginia, to pretend to be normal until he could strike again.

Over the years, they elaborated a detailed plan of convincing Rae to follow through with the suicide pact. Kenan had thought it should only be those two to visit the cabin this weekend, but Tobey changed his mind. If the group tagged along, then he could have his fun too. The perfect place where no one could escape.

The only catch: Tobey couldn't lay a finger on Rae. Kenan didn't care who he tormented or tortured as long as it broke Rae down emotionally to the point she'd be ready to die. But he absolutely could not hurt her physically. Kenan was lucky to have a best friend like Tobey, someone who helped his dreams become a reality.

Rae's body trembled. She pleaded, "Please, Kenan, I don't want to die."

"You can't just change your mind. How selfish." He pulled the gun out of his belt buckle. Rae gasped. "I guess we won't be committing suicide the easy way, always picking the hard way, making things difficult for yourself." He took a step towards Rae.

"Wait. Please. No, Kenan, please. You need help." She stretched her arms out to keep distance between them. She took a step back but went up against the wall. Trapped. Nowhere else to go. Well, unless she opened the window and went down the water pipe like Tobey had done.

So clever. It worked out by Kenan stalling the group to give Tobey enough time to shoot Logan and climb back up. Kenan knew Brady only looked out for himself, so wouldn't dare enter the room with Tobey *crying*. Too much work to comfort him.

Kenan sighed. "Are there any questions for me?"

"Why?" Rae placed her hand over her heart.

"I already told you. Come on, Rae. Don't you want to know something exciting? Like how did Tobey kill Logan? Wasn't that awesome? I didn't know he had good aim like that. Sorry that Logan's brains splattered all over you. I tried to pull you back, but you're so stubborn." Rae cried, trying to cover her face with her hands, so Kenan talked louder. "Rae, do you have any questions?"

Since she wasn't the least bit curious, he might as well end their lives now. He took another step toward her.

"Please, I don't want to die."

"Then ask me a question."

"How did we get back here?"

"I drove. The car was drivable if you knew how to fix it. I was going to carry you here, but time is of the essence since you radioed help. I knew I should have smashed that stupid thing last night."

Rae shook her head. "Kenan, please. You need help. Let RL sign the deed then we'll get closure. We'll never have to come back here again."

"Come on, Rae. Deep down, you know RL never existed. I set up a fake account with a second phone, making sure to dial the number when no one was looking. It was the only thing I could think of to get you here." Kenan smiled. "We'll be seeing all our friends soon. I know you want this, just as much as you wanted it when you were fifteen."

It was time.

"I love you, Rae." Kenan also loved their parents and couldn't wait to reunite with them. Rae would be happy too; she was just in denial about it.

He sprinted towards her, grabbed her by the waist, and they flew out the third floor window.

Total darkness.

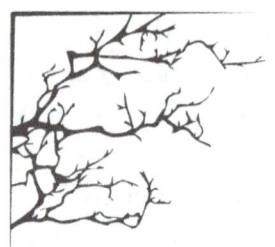

# Epilogue

Detective Brown examined the crime scene; he felt disgusted to the point he needed to throw up. The sight was sinister. Who was capable of a killing spree like this? His stomach ached and a knot formed in his throat. He had a young daughter and couldn't even imagine if something tragic like this happened to her.

There was a strangled woman lying on the porch, half decapitated due to the animals feasting off her rotten remains. A girl and guy lay beside each other, she on her back and he on his stomach. She had a dread expression as if she had screamed "No" while he looked at peace, almost as if smiling. They had landed on stakes. If not for that, probably would've still died instantly from plummeting at that height. Detective Brown assumed they were thrown out the window because of all the glass covering the ground.

Jeeps were filled with bags and suitcases, so they had tried to leave. Unfortunately, not in time. If he thought it looked bad outside, it looked even worse inside. One of their own, Ranger Kirby, stabbed upstairs, a woman gutted in bed, and a guy's face destroyed by an arrow.

Detective Brown shivered, kneeled down to get a closer view of the guy and girl before the coroner would put their bodies into the black bags. They looked so familiar that he couldn't quite put his finger on it, then it hit him all at once.

They had been brother and sister tortured in this cabin many years ago.

Detective Brown fell back, landing on his butt.

"Sir, are you okay?"

In a daze, he turned to face the police officer. "Yeah, I tripped." He got back on his feet and dusted himself off. He whispered, "I'll make the sick fucks pay for what they did to you."

Detective Alvarez stood beside him. "This place has to be cursed. A tragedy like this happened ten years ago."

"It took the town a very long time to move on."

162

"And now this."

Detective Brown shook his head in anger. "We'll get the sick fucks like we did ten years ago."

His partner nodded. "Maybe friends were here for a getaway, and robbers came in. Someone was able to call for help, but Ranger Kirby was killed too."

Call for help. That's the only reason the police knew to come to this address; a young lady had radioed them. Was she still alive? Had she got away from this hell?

As if there wasn't enough on their plates, the cops searching through the bags found nine driver licenses total. Where were the other four people? Was it a fight gone deadly wrong and the other friends ran after murdering these people? A deadly feud?

That theory wasn't able to form in his mind for too long because Detective Brown kept getting dispatched. First, they found a body hung from a tree. Then, one by one, three were mentioned being dead throughout the woods.

Both detectives shared a worried look. He couldn't stop covering the case until it was solved. The victims' families deserved to get closure for their kids.

Forensics bagging up evidence from the ground, officers canvassing the area for any clues all resembled a surreal blur. This would definitely be a high profile case, and he couldn't wait to get these kids' stories told. They deserved that much for all the torture they had went through.

*Crackle. Crackle. Snap. Snap.*

The detectives and officers quickly turned around, pulling out their revolvers, aiming at a potential suspect. It was only a deer. Everyone, except Detective Brown, relaxed and put their guns down. They laughed about how they got startled so easily. But Detective Brown couldn't relax. There was a killer, or possibly killers, out there who needed to rot in prison until he, or they, received the death penalty. No way could Detective Brown put his guard down. The killer, or killers, could still be out there ready to attack again.

Was this a one time incident or did they have a serial killer on their hands?

## THE END

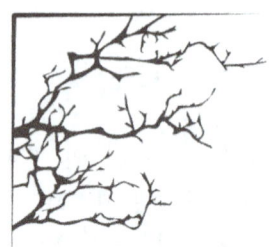

# About The Author

Yawatta Hosby resides in the eastern panhandle of West Virginia. She teaches creative writing through the Adult Community Education program, and she enjoys connecting with other writers through blogging. With a desire to escape every day life, she creates short stories, novellas, and novels. She's always had a fascination with psychology, so she likes to focus on the inner-struggles within her characters. Yawatta is also an avid reader, favorite genres: mystery, thriller, horror, and women's fiction.

She'd love to hear from her fans and readers:

Blog: http://yawattahosby.wordpress.com

Twitter: http://www.twitter.com/yawatta_hosby

Author Page on Facebook: http://www.facebook.com/YawattaHosby

# Don't miss out!

Visit the website below and you can sign up to receive emails whenever Yawatta Hosby publishes a new book. There's no charge and no obligation.

https://books2read.com/r/B-A-LFIB-AUCX

BOOKS 2 READ

Connecting independent readers to independent writers.

# Also by Yawatta Hosby

One By One
Something's Amiss
Twisted Obsession
Six Plus One
Perfect Little Murder
Two Book Boxset
Urban Legends

Watch for more at yawattahosbysbooks.wordp.